Acknowledged as one of the great Latin American writers of this century, Juan Carlos Onetti was born in Montevideo, Uruguay in 1909. For many years he worked as a journalist in Buenos Aires. His novels include *The Well*, *No Man's Life*, *Brief Life* and his best known work, *The Shipyard*, written in 1961. Onetti now lives in Madrid.

THE SHIPYARD

Juan Carlos Onetti

Translated by Nick Caistor

SERPENT'S
TAIL

Series editors: Pete Ayrton and Martin Chalmers

Library of Congress Catalog Card Number: 91-61205

British Library Cataloguing in Publication Data

Onetti, Juan Carlos *1909–*
  The shipyard.
  I. Title   II. (El Astillero) *English*
  863.64 (F)

  ISBN 1-85242-191-6

First published as *El Astillero*
Copyright © Juan Carlos Onetti, 1961
Translation copyright © 1992 by Serpent's Tail

This edition first published in 1992 by
Serpent's Tail, 4 Blackstock Mews, London N4
and 401 West Broadway #2, New York, NY10012

Set in 10½/14pt Galliard by Contour Typesetters, Southall, London
Printed in Great Britain by Hartnoll's Ltd. of Bodmin, Cornwall

To Luis Batlle Berres

SANTA MARIA I

At the time five years ago when the Governor decided to banish Larsen (alias The Bodysnatcher) from the province, some joker prophesied he would be back one day to resume his hundred-day reign: that fascinating, controversial (though now all but forgotten) chapter in our history. Few heard the prophecy. Even Larsen, his strength sapped by his downfall, under police escort, probably forgot the phrase immediately, despairing of ever returning among us.

Yet one morning five years after that episode, Larsen appeared at the stop for buses from Colón. He rested his suitcase on the ground while he pulled down his silk shirt-cuffs, then with that rolling gait of his slowly made his entry into Santa Maria, just after the rain had stopped, maybe heavier than before, more squat, apparently tamed, no different from anyone else.

He had a drink at the bar of the Berna, calmly following the barman's eyes until he won a silent acknowledgement. He had lunch there on his own, surrounded by truck drivers in their check shirts. (By now, they were competing with the railway to take freight to El Rosario and the coast towns of the north; they all looked as if they had been born this way — sturdy, in their twenties, loud, and empty of any past — by the side of the macadam road inaugurated a few months earlier.) For his coffee with brandy, Larsen moved to a table close to the door and window.

Many people swear they saw him that lunchtime in the dying days of autumn. Some claim he looked like his old self resurrected in the exaggerated way, almost caricatured, that he was trying to recapture the indolence, the irony, the sparse disdain of the postures and expressions he had employed five years before; they recall how keen he was to be noticed and identified, his two fingers ready to rise jerkily to the brim of his hat at the slightest hint of greeting, at any look which remotely suggested surprise at seeing him again. Others on the contrary remember him as indifferent, hostile, resting his elbows on the table, a cigarette dangling from his mouth, parallel to the drenched Artigas Avenue, as he peered into the faces of those coming in for no other reason than to keep a personal tally of loyalties and betrayals, acknowledging either response with the same easy, fleeting smile, the same involuntary twitch of the mouth.

He paid for his lunch, tipped over-generously as usual, then went upstairs to his room in the pension over the Berna. After a siesta, more truly himself, less conspicuous now he had left his suitcase behind, he began to explore Santa Maria, unaware of his noisy footsteps, offering the appearance of a bored stranger to all the people, doorways, shop windows he encountered. He walked round the four sides and two diagonals of the square as if trying to solve the problem of how to get from A to B using every possible route without going the same way twice; he paced up and down outside the freshly painted black railings of the church; went into the chemist's (still owned by Barthé) more slowly than ever, more typical of himself, more watchful, to weigh himself, buy soap and toothpaste, to study, like an unexpected photo of a friend, the bit of cardboard announcing: "the chemist will be out until five p.m."

Then he set out on an expedition further afield. His body swayed even more as he walked three or four blocks down towards where the coast road and the one to La Colonia cross, along the neglected street with the little corner house with sky blue balconies, now rented by Morentz the dentist. Later on, he was spotted near Redondo's mill, his shoes sunk in the wet grass, leaning against a tree for a smoke; at Mantero's dairy he clapped his hands, bought a glass of milk and some bread, would give no straight answers to the people trying to place him ("he was sad, aged, looking for a fight; he flashed his money as if we might think he'd run off without paying.") In all likelihood he drifted around La Colonia for a few hours, before turning up again at half past seven in the bar of the Plaza hotel, which had not been one of his haunts when he had lived in Santa Maria. Throughout the evening he continued the display of aggression and curiosity already noted at midday in the Berna.

He engaged in friendly banter with the barman (with a tacit, sustained allusion to a topic dead and buried for five years) about recipes for cocktails, the size of the chunks of ice, the length of the spoons for stirring them. Perhaps he was expecting Marcos and his friends to show up; he glanced at Dr Diaz Grey but made no attempt to greet him. He paid his new bill, pushed a tip across the counter, then climbed awkwardly but confidently down from the bar stool. He walked along the strip of linoleum, with his calculated swagger, short and rolling, sure in the knowledge that the truth, however wasted away, emanated from the tapping of his heels and was conveyed in an insolent, direct manner to the air, to others.

He left the hotel and it is almost certain he crossed the square to sleep in his room at the Berna. But no one living in the town remembers seeing him again until he had been back a fortnight. That was a Sunday, when we all saw Larsen outside the church at the end of eleven o'clock mass, guileful, old, shaved and powdered, clutching a tiny bunch of violets to his chest. We all saw how Jeremias Petrus' daughter — his only, idiot, unmarried child — passed by Larsen, dragging along her fuming, hunchback father

3

— how she was on the verge of smiling at the flowers before she snapped her eyes shut in bewildered terror, then walked on, turning her pouting lips, her restless, apparently squinting, eyes to the ground.

THE SHIPYARD I

It must have been by chance, because Larsen cannot have known. Of all those who lived in Santa Maria, Larsen's only possible correspondent during his five years' exile was Vazquez, the newsagent; and there is no proof that Vazquez could even write. Even were he able to, it seems highly unlikely that the ruined shipyard, the rise and fall of Jeremias Petrus, his villa with its marble statues, or the idiot girl, would have been topics Froilan Vazquez chose to write about. Or perhaps it was not chance, but destiny. Larsen's nose, his intuition, working to fulfil his fate, brought him back to Santa Maria to carry out this childish revenge of reclaiming the streets and bars of the city he loathed. Then they guided him to the house with its marble statues, its leaky gutters, overgrown lawns, to the tangle of electric cables in the shipyard.

According to reports, two days after his return, Larsen left the hotel early and walked slowly — his swagger, the click of his heels, his weight, all exaggerated to those who had known him before, as was his condescending expression, which spoke of favours done, thanks refused — down the deserted river bank to the fishermen's jetty. He unfolded his newspaper to sit on, gazed at the hazy outline of the far shore, the trucks coming and going in the Enduro canning factory yard, the working boats and those which emerged, long, light and mysteriously propelled forward, from the

5

Rowing Club. Seated on the damp stones of the jetty, he ate a lunch of fried fish, bread, and wine, sold to him by insistent barefoot boys still in their summer rags. He watched the ferry arrive and drop off its passengers, glancing absent-mindedly at their faces; he yawned, plucked the pearl pin from his black tie to clean his teeth with. He thought of a few deaths, and this brought back memories, wry smiles, proverbs, bungling attempts to change other people's destinies. By then it was almost two o'clock; he stood up, ran two saliva-covered fingers down his trouser creases, picked up the newspaper, (the previous day's Buenos Aires edition) then mingled with the people heading down the ramp to board the white, covered launch for the journey back up-river.

Larsen spent the trip reading from the paper he had already read in bed that morning. He sat with one leg crossed over the other, oblivious to the swaying of the boat. His hat was pulled down over one eye, his face raised in a blank glare aimed as much at concealing the effort it took him to read as to ward off any chance of being seen and recognised. He got off at a landing stage known as Puerto Astillero, behind a fat old woman carrying a basket and a sleeping child, as he might have disembarked anywhere along the river.

Unheeding, Larsen toiled up the damp earth beside the broad green-stained planks overgrown with weeds that served as steps. He glanced at the two rusty cranes, the grey cube of the shipyard building looming up out of the flat landscape, its huge lettering so rotten that it seemed like some hoarse giant reduced to whispering the words JEREMIAS PETRUS LTD. Although it was late in the afternoon, there were two lighted windows in the office building. Larsen went up past wretched shacks, wire fences smothered in climbing plants, past the barking of dogs, past women who leant on their hoes or paused at their washing to cast him furtive glances, waiting.

Dirt or mud streets, unmarked by vehicles, sectioned by the

promise of light from brand-new lampposts. At his back, the incongruous cement building, the slipway empty of boats or workmen, the ancient iron cranes that would surely grind themselves to dust if ever anyone tried to start them up. The sky had clouded over completely; the air was still, expectant.

"What a squalid hole," Larsen spat; then gave a short laugh, standing there alone in a corner of four tongues of earth: a heavy, small, aimless man, crouched there against the years he had lived in Santa Maria, against his return, against the low, full clouds, against misfortune.

He turned left, walked on another two blocks, entered the Belgrano: bar, restaurant, hotel, general store. In other words, he went into a store that had rope sandals, bottles and ploughshares in the window, a sign lit by a simple bulb over the door, a floor that was half earthen, half coloured tiles; into a store he would soon learn to call "Belgrano's". He sat at a table to ask for something or other, lodging, cigarettes they did not sell, a drink of anisette with soda. All there was left for him to do was to wait for the rain, to put up with hearing it and seeing it — through the window-pane with its whitewashed letters recommending a treatment for mange — for as long as it beat on the welcoming earth and the tin roof. Then finally it would be the end, he could renounce any faith in his presentiments, could accept once and for all an end to belief, accept old age.

He ordered another anisette with soda, carefully mixing his drink while his mind strayed back to lost years and pernod, the real thing, when suddenly the door opened and the woman almost ran up to the counter. Larsen linked the earlier sound of horses with this tall-booted figure who was talking urgently to the store owner, and with the second woman, plump, docile, Indian-looking, who quietly closed the door, pushing it to gently against the rising wind, then went and stood patiently, obsequiously, yet with a threat of domination, in control, behind the first.

Larsen knew at once that something unexpected could happen; all that mattered to him was the woman in boots. Everything would have to be done through the other one, through her complicity, her grudging acquiescence. This one, the maid — standing a pace behind her mistress, her stumpy legs wide apart, hands crossed over her stomach, a dark scarf wrapped round her head, her face expressionless but for a frozen smile, deliberately void of meaning, could not stir him from his lassitude: he knew her type by heart, they were easily classified, reproduced without any real differences, as though mass produced, like an animal, simple or complicated, dog or cat, time would tell. He turned his attention to the other woman, who was still laughing and beat at the edge of the tin counter with her riding-crop. She was tall, blonde; at some moments thirty years old, at others forty.

Her clear eyes retained something of her childhood when she narrowed them to look round — a flashing, defiant gleam that was instantly quenched. There was also something child-like about her flat chest, her man's shirt and the small velvet bow at her neck; and more definite reminders in her long legs, her trim boyish buttocks that barely filled her jodhpurs. She had big buck teeth and whenever she laughed her face shook, astonished and watchful at the same time, as though she were ridding herself of her laughter, watching it split off from her, white, gleaming, excessive; watching it recede and die in a second, melting away without trace or echo on to the bar, the owner's shoulders, the cobwebs which linked the bottles on the shelf behind him. Her long flaxen hair was combed back and tied with another black velvet ribbon.

"Well, I'll be damned," Larsen said. He waved a finger at the waiter for another anis, smiled as he realised that a gentle rain had begun to fall on roof and street, accompanying him, sharing his secret, knowing.

The long strands of lustreless hair, its darker ends twisting up, hung ageless against the woman's shirt collar. Her pale face peered from under the lily-shaped, keyhole-shaped metallic frame of hair, a face with recent wrinkles, revealing its wear and tear, its paint, its past; then there was her raucous laugh about nothing, a laugh as inevitable as a hiccough, a cough, or a sneeze.

No one else was sitting at the tables; the women would have to pass by him when they left, look at him. But the moment called for something else, another way of being looked at. Larsen straightened his tie, plumped the silk handkerchief in his top pocket, and walked slowly up to the bar. He screened the woman behind his left shoulder as he smiled politely at the owner.

"Don't think I'm complaining about the anis," he said in a deep, ringing voice. "I know that these days . . . But don't you have a better brand?" The proprietor said he did not, but ventured a name. Larsen shook his head, only slightly disappointed; he was listening to the silence of the woman beside him, to the "well it's time to go, it's started to rain," from the maid in the background, from her remote but present depths. Larsen tried out some foreign brands, without success; his dry monotone showed he was expecting as much, and was merely going through the motions.

"It's all right, it doesn't matter. Let me take a look at the labels."

He leaned on the counter, still smiling indulgently as he slowly read the labels on the bottles behind the bar. The woman laughed again, but he did not want to look at her; something told him this was it, the patter of the rain spoke of vengeance and of worth being recognised, proclaimed the necessity of a final deed to make sense of all the lost years.

"But I'm sure, señorita, that everything will be all right. It's all a question of time," the proprietor said.

She laughed once more, her body bent over until the laughter had been expelled, been transformed, absorbed, by the languid, solemn, inflexible rain.

"Wait. You're afraid of getting wet," she said to the servant, without turning round. It was impossible to tell who she was looking at; her eyes darted from side to side, before coming to rest a couple of inches above the proprietor's head. "He says everything will be all right. He came up with the money, the idea and the plans; he did the work. Governments come and go, agree, say he's right; but they come and go, and it isn't sorted out." She laughed again, waited resignedly for the laughter to detach itself from her protruding teeth, rolling her eyes apologetically, imploringly. "Ever since I was a child. Now it seems certain, a matter of weeks. I'm not worried for me, but every morning I go with her to church to pray to God that just once things come right, before he is too old. It would be so sad."

"No, no," the proprietor said. "It will sort itself out, and soon." Leaning on the bar, Larsen stared at the servant, a look of friendly surprise on his face; he smiled a narrow smile until, swaying forward, she began to blink, parted her lips. She took a step, still looking at him, and touched the other woman's shirt.

"Let's go, it's raining and it'll soon be dark," she said.

Without looking, Larsen quickly picked the riding crop up from the bar and, courteous and silent, offered it to the woman with the long hair, the laugh and the boots. He waited until they had gone, watched them mount their horses through the yellow, desolate view from the store window, then renewed his sterile conversation about makes of anis with the owner, offered him a drink, asked no questions and lied in reply to the ones put to him.

Night was drawing in, and the rain had eased to a drizzle by the time he stirred to catch the last ferry to Santa Maria. He walked slowly, oblivious to the rain dripping from the trees on to him, down to the darkness and the solitude of the quayside. He did not want to think ahead, to admit anything. The woman in the riding habit came to his mind; he conjured up all her impetuosity, her weariness.

THE SUMMERHOUSE I

A fortnight later, as we have said, Larsen appeared on the church steps at the end of Mass, timidly offering a bunch of early violets that he had been clutching to his chest. He reappeared in public that Sunday noon, inviting ridicule, doing nothing to defend himself from it. He stood there, stiff and calm, his bulk straining against the dark, tight-fitting overcoat, indifferent, alone, yielding like a statue to everyone's gaze, to the bad weather, to the birds, to the spiteful words they would never dare say to his face. This was in June, around St John's Day, when Angelica Ines, Petrus' daughter, was spending a few days with relatives in Santa Maria near la Colonia.

Then he appeared (by now back in Puerto Astillero and installed in a sordid room at Belgrano's) outside the iron gate where the initials J and P were discreetly entwined. He walked through the weed-choked garden surrounding the house that Petrus had built on fourteen cement pillars on the riverbank near the shipyard. He spent long evenings exchanging ambiguous, nostalgic, professional whispers with the maid. She was thirty, had been brought up by Petrus' now deceased wife, and was wasting her life in a game of adoration, fellow-feeling, domination, revenge, in which "the child" and her imbecility were at one and the same time the object, the incentive, and the opponent. Larsen obtained a series of almost identical meetings, so similar they might have been taken for boring repetitions of the same nagging failure; meetings whose charm came in equal measure from the distance, the luminosity of what had now turned into a dry winter, the slight incongruity of Angelica Ines Petrus' long white dresses, the dramatic slowness with which Larsen freed his head from his black hat, held it for a few seconds, a few inches, above his enthralled, candid, artificial smile.

Then came their first real meeting, a talk in the garden when Larsen was needlessly and unknowingly humiliated, when he was given a token of greater humiliations to come, of ultimate failure, a warning light, an invitation to give up that he was unable to interpret. He did not realise he was facing an entirely new challenge in her stolen glances, her half-hidden smile as she bit her fingernails; his age and over-confidence led him to believe that an ample and rich experience makes one infallible.

Old man Petrus was in Buenos Aires, fabricating written defences with his lawyer or seeking out proof of his pioneering vision, of his faith in the nation's greatness, or scurrying wretchedly between ministers and bank managers, humble, indignant. The maid Josefina had agreed, after being besieged for two nights and after the surprise present of a silk shawl, after countless declarations of love and its torments, not exclusively inspired by Angelica Ines but — in a vague, broad sense — by all women who had ever sighed on this earth, with the special inclusion of her, Josefina, the maid.

So it was that at five one afternoon a black-suited Larsen made his way along the eucalyptus-lined street, ironed, clean, dignified, a box of pastries dangling from one finger, protecting his shiny shoes from the last rain's puddles, heavy with guile and self-confidence, avid but restrained.

"Right on time," Josefina said at the gate, laughing at him with a hint of reproach. She was wearing a new apron, full of flower patterns and starch.

Larsen touched the brim of his hat and offered her the box.

"I brought this," he murmured apologetically.

She did not stretch out a finger to take the box by the blue bow, as Bodysnatcher had been expecting; instead, she held it against her curving thigh like a book, looked the man up and down, from his tender smile to the spotless tips of his patent leather shoes.

"I wish I hadn't agreed to this," she said. "But now she's waiting for you. Don't forget what I told you. You have tea, then you go, and you respect her."

"Of course, sweetheart," Larsen agreed. He looked her in the eye, and his face darkened. "Whatever you say. If you prefer, I won't go beyond the door. You're in charge."

She stared at him again, at his tiny, calm eyes that spoke only of respect and obedience. She shrugged, and walked back through the garden. Hat in hand, watching her hips, her firm footsteps, Larsen followed her warily, not sure whether he had been invited.

The grass had been left to grow as it pleased for at least a year; the tree trunks were spotted white and green with dull dampness. In the centre of the garden — it was enough now for Larsen to be guided by the sound of her regular footsteps, the clicking sound as her legs cut like blades through the weeds — there was a round pond, protected by a low moss-covered wall about a metre high, with more dead stalks poking through its cracks. Near the pond, beyond it, stood a summerhouse, also round, and made of wooden laths that had once been painted navy blue, which created diamond-shaped spaces where they crossed. Behind the summer-house stood the dirty white and grey concrete villa, built like a cube, with windows on all sides, and clumsily raised on its pillars far above the level of any possible flooding from the river. Everywhere in the garden, stained marble statues of naked women glowed white from under the foliage. "They're letting it fall into ruin," Larsen said to himself disapprovingly; "Two hundred thousand pesos at the very least, and who knows how much land there is behind, between the house and the river." Josefina skirted the pond; Larsen followed meekly, glancing at the stagnant water, the bedraggled plants floating on the surface, the cherub crouched in the middle.

The woman stopped at the door to the summerhouse, casually motioned him in. Disappointed, Larsen smiled and nodded, took off his hat and walked over to the cement table inside, surrounded by iron chairs, and covered with an embroidered cloth set with cups, a vase of violets, plates with cakes and biscuits.

"Make yourself at home. She'll be here in a minute. It's not a cold afternoon," Josefina said without looking at him, swinging the box in her hand all the while.

"Thanks. Everything looks perfect," he nodded again at her, at her squat hurried form as it brushed past the wooden walls and left.

Trying to analyse why he felt cheated, Larsen hung his hat on a nail, drew a finger across one of the iron chairs, then spread his handkerchief before sitting down.

It was five in the afternoon at the end of a sunny winter's day. Through the rough wooden slats daubed with blue paint, Larsen contemplated diamond-shaped fragments of the declining hour, of the landscape, saw the shadows lengthen as if they were fleeing, the grass lawn flatten though there was no wind. A damp smell, chill and penetrating, a smell evoking night and closed eyes, came from the pond. On the other side, the house loomed above its slender cement prisms, above the gaping, purple-tinged darkness, above piles of summer mattresses and garden chairs, a hose pipe, a bicycle. Screwing up one eye to get a better view, Larsen saw the house as the empty shape of a heaven he coveted and had been promised; as the gates of a city he longed to enter once and for all, where he could spend the rest of his days enjoying revenge without suffering, sensuality without effort, an unheeded narcissistic power.

He muttered a curse then put on a smile as he stood up to greet the two women. He was convinced that an expression of slight surprise would suffice, and was able to profit from it later, when they began their conversation: "I was waiting here for you, thinking of you, and I had almost forgotten where I was and that you were going to come; so that when you appeared it was as if what I was thinking were real." He almost insisted on serving the tea, but understood just in time, as he was rising from his seat, that in the complicated world of the summerhouse, politeness could be expressed passively. Angelica Ines would begin a phrase — eyes rolling like a cornered animal, on her guard, but not really afraid, accustomed long since to harassment and dangers — and think to round it off, make it comprehensible and memorable, with two short guffaws. Then she would sit for a moment looking totally blank, eyes and mouth wide open as if she used them to hear with, until the two notes of her laughter seemed to have finally dissolved into thin air. At that point, she became serious again, searching for traces of her laugh in Larsen's face, then turned away.

Beyond the diamonds of the summerhouse, distant but present, her figure sliced in two by the weeds, Joesefina was scolding the dog, tying up the stakes round the roses. The still undefined problem lay inside the summerhouse, in the white, submissive face framed by a mass of hair, the plump white arms that began to stir, then stopped and fell back before any confession was complete. There was the mauve dress, billowing out at the waist and reaching right down to the buckles on her shoes, embroidered across the bosom and shoulders. And inside and out, above them but clinging to Larsen's stout, alert body, there was the winter evening, the taut, decrepit air.

"When the old house was flooded," she said, "mummy was no longer with us, it was at night, we began to carry everything upstairs to the bedrooms, everybody took their favourite things, it was like an adventure. The horse was more frightened than any of us, the hens all drowned, the boys began to live on their rowing boats. Daddy was furious, but he was never scared. The boys rowed past in between the trees; they wanted to bring us food and to take us with them. We had enough food. In the new house, it doesn't matter if the water rises. The boys would row past, they didn't care at all, they came from all around in their boats, waving to us, waving shirts."

"Guess when," Larsen said in the summerhouse. "You won't, not in a million years, because you weren't interested. I was in Belgrano's quite by chance; the hotel a block from the shipyard. I had no idea what to do with my life; I boarded a ferry and got off where fancy took me. It started to rain, so I went into the bar. That's how it was when you came in. Ever since then I've felt the need to see you, to talk to you. For no reason: I'm not from these parts. But I didn't want to leave before I had seen you, talked to you. Now at last I can breathe again: I can look at you, say whatever I like. I don't know what life still holds in store for me; but meeting you is reward enough. I can see you, look at you."

Josefina hit the dog, making it yelp. The two rushed into the summerhouse, the woman smiling and panting as she took in Angelica Ines' face, Larsen's doleful profile, the plates forgotten on the cement table.

"I'm not making any demands," Larsen said, out loud. "But I'd like to see you again. And thank you, sincerely, for everything."

He clicked his heels, bowed to them. As he went to recover his hat, Petrus' daughter stood up laughing. Larsen bent forward again to pick up his handkerchief from the seat.

"It's night already," Josefina whispered. She leaned against the doorpost, staring at the hand she was holding out for the dog to jump at. "I'll show you out."

Deaf and blind, led on by the maid's body, Larsen lost himself among the repeated prophecies of the cold, the jagged tug of the weeds, the mournful light, the distant barking.

Reckless, rejuvenated, Larsen cupped Josefina's chin in his hand under the J and P of the gate, leaned down to kiss her.

"Thanks, my love," he said. "I know how to show my gratitude."

She put a hand over his mouth.

"Whoa there," she said absently, as if to a tame horse.

THE SHIPYARD II

It is not known how Jeremias Petrus and Larsen came to meet.

It is, however, beyond doubt that it was Larsen who arranged their meeting, possibly with the help of Poetters, the owner of Belgrano's; it is unthinkable that Larsen should ask that kind of favour of anyone in Santa Maria. It is also worth bearing in mind that the shipyard had been deprived of a General Manager's attention and initiative for the six months prior to this.

At any rate, the meeting took place one day at noon in the shipyard, so that not even then was Larsen able to enter the house on cement pillars.

"Galvez and Kunz," Petrus said, pointing to them. "Our administration and technical department. Loyal supporters."

Ironic, hostile, teamed up to disconcert him, the bald younger man and the older one with a mane of black hair shook hands coolly, then looked straight at Petrus and spoke.

"We'll finish the inventory tomorrow, sir," said Kunz, the older man.

"Checking it," Galvez corrected him, with an over-sweet smile, rubbing the tips of his fingers together. "So far, there's not so much as a screw missing."

"Not even a staple," Kunz asserted.

Petrus stood propped against the desk, his black hat still in place, cupping one hand to his ear to hear better. He squinted at the paneless window and the cold light of the afternoon beyond it; his lips pressed shut, he nodded nervously and pompously as each new thought flitted across his mind.

Larsen again gauged the hostility and mockery on the immobile faces of the two waiting men. To challenge and repay hatred might give his life a meaning, a habit, some pleasure; almost anything would be better than this roof with its leaky sheet iron, these dusty, lopsided desks, the heaps of files and folders stacked against the walls, the thorny vines winding themselves round the iron bars of the gaping window, the exasperating, hysterical farce of work, enterprise, and prosperity that the furniture spoke of (though now it was vanquished by use and moths, rushing towards its destiny as firewood); the documents made filthy by rain, sun and footprints, the rolls of blueprints stacked in pyramids all torn and tattered on the walls.

"Exactly," Petrus said at last in his asthmatic whine. "We must be able to offer the Creditors Committee regular reassurance, without being asked, that their interests are being faithfully looked after. We have to keep going until justice is done; to go on working — something I have always done — as though nothing had happened. A captain should go down with his ship; but we, my friends, are not going down. We are adrift and listing, but this is not yet a shipwreck." A whistling sound came from his chest as he spoke these last words, his eyebrows shot up proudly and expectantly; he flashed his yellow teeth, scratched his hat brim. "Make sure you finish checking the stock tomorrow please, gentlemen. Señor Larsen . . ."

Slowly and calculatingly, Larsen stared out the two faces as they said goodbye to him with matching smiles that not only emphasised their obscure mockery but unwittingly demonstrated an inevitable complicity of caste. Then, as he followed Petrus' figure out of the room, Larsen consciously, bearing no grudge and hardly any sorrow, breathed in the air reeking of dampness, the filthy papers, winter, toilet, remoteness, ruin and deceit. He did not need to turn round to hear Galvez and Kunz proclaim loudly:

"The grand old man of the shipyard. The great self-made man."

Then to hear Kunz or Galvez respond, mimicking Petrus' falsely ceremonious voice: "As all you shareholders know, I am a true pioneer."

Petrus and he passed through two doorless offices — dust, disorder, a palpable desolation, the tangled cables of a telephone switchboard, the insistent, incredible blue of the ferroprussiate plans, identical pieces of furniture, their legs splintered — before Petrus skirted a huge oval-shaped table with nothing more on it than a layer of dust, two telephones and two worn, unused green blotters.

He hung up his hat and offered Larsen a seat. For a moment, Petrus sat lost in thought, his bushy eyebrows knit together, his hands open on the table. Then he smiled unexpectedly between his long, flat sideburns, staring into Larsen's eyes with no trace of enjoyment, offering only his long yellowing teeth and just possibly his pride at still having them. Shivering with cold, unable to rouse himself to indignation or astonishment, Larsen found himself nodding agreement during the pauses in Petrus' immortal speech which months or years before Galvez, Kunz, and dozens of other wretched men had listened to hopefully, gratefully — all of them now dispersed, disappeared, some of them dead, all of them phantoms — finding in the drawn-out, carefully articulated sentences, the variable and fascinating offer, a corroboration of God's existence, of their good fortune, of justice that was tardy but true.

"Over thirty million, señor Larsen. And that figure does not include the enormous increase in value of some of our stock in the past few years, or other items which can still be salvaged, such as kilometres of roads which can be converted into saleable lots, and the first section of the railway. I am just mentioning what is on hand at this very moment, what could be sold immediately to produce that amount. The building, the scrap iron from the ships, machinery, and spare parts that you can inspect in the shed whenever you wish. I shall give señor Kunz instructions to that effect. There is every indication that the judge is about to lift the bankruptcy order, and once we are free of the bureaucratic, crippling financial control imposed by the Creditors Committee, we can set about reviving the company with new vigour. I know I can call on the necessary funds, all I have to do is choose. That is where your services will be important to me. I am an excellent judge of men and I am sure I will not regret my choice. But it is essential you waste no time getting to know the company. The post I am offering you is that of General Manager of Jeremias Petrus Ltd. It carries with it a great deal of responsibility, and will be no easy task. As far as your remuneration is concerned, I await your proposal as soon as you feel you are in a position to appreciate what the company expects of you as regards loyalty, intelligence, and trustworthiness."

All through his speech, Petrus had kept his hands in front of his face, the fingertips pressed together; he now dropped them to the table again, showed his teeth once more.

"I'll make my proposal, as you say," Larsen calmly replied, "once I have studied the situation. It's not something to rush into." He kept back the figure that had been forming in his mind for several days, from the moment that Angelica Ines had confirmed, gawping at him in disbelief, in the first stirrings of love and esteem, that her father was thinking of offering him a position at the shipyard, a steady, lucrative post that would tempt señor Larsen to stay, a job and a future that were more than a match for the offers from Buenos Aires that señor Larsen was considering.

Jeremias Petrus stood up, reached for his hat. Preoccupied, reluctant to accept any renewal of faith, halfheartedly rebelling against the protective feeling offered by the old man's hunched shoulders, Larsen escorted him back through the two empty rooms to the freezing, bright main office.

"The lads have gone to eat," Petrus said indulgently, a faint smile flicking across his face. "But we shouldn't waste time. Come back this afternoon and see them. You are now the General Manager. I have to go to Buenos Aires at midday. We can settle the details later."

Larsen was left on his own. Hands behind his back, he began to walk round the enormous empty office, treading carefully among piles of blueprints and documents, mounds of dust, creaking boards. There had once been glass panes in the windows, each pair of torn wires had once plugged into a telephone, twenty or thirty men had sat bent over their desks while a girl unerringly handled the switchboard ("Petrus Limited, good morning"), and other girls sashayed over to the filing cabinets. The old man made the women wear grey overalls. Perhaps they believed it was he who forced them to remain spinsters and not to cause any scandal. The young men in the Dispatch Department sent off three hundred letters a day, at the very least. In the background, invisible, half believed in, as old as he was now, just as shrunken and self-assured, Petrus. Thirty million.

The lads, Kunz and Galvez, were having lunch at Belgrano's. If Larsen had paid heed to his hunger that midday, if he had not preferred to fast among symbols, in an atmosphere of epilogue which he unknowingly heightened and loved — with the intensity of that love, sense of rediscovery and peace of mind with which one breathes the air of one's homeland — he might perhaps have saved himself, or at least have continued to destroy himself without having to admit it, without his failure becoming so evident, public, so gloated over.

On several occasions since the afternoon when he had unthinkingly disembarked in Puerto Astillero behind a fat lady struggling with a basket and a sleeping child, he had felt with foreboding the greedy jaws of some obscure trap. Now he was caught, but could not name it, could not admit he had travelled, made plans, used up smiles, acts of cunning and patience only to fall into it, to settle into a last refuge that was this desperate and absurd.

If he had searched through the empty building to find the staircase — at the foot of which, by some miracle, a smiling metal nymph was still flying, her garments and hair moulded stiffly round her by a sea breeze, effortlessly holding aloft an outsize torch with a twisted glass flame — he would almost certainly have gone to Belgrano's for lunch. In that case, all that happened twenty-four hours later, during the next lunch-time, when unbeknown to himself he had already made his irrevocable choice, would have happened now, before he had accepted his own perdition.

Because the following midday Larsen walked into Belgrano's and saw Galvez and Kunz turn to look at him from the table where they were eating together; they did not ask him to sit with them, or call him over. But they kept their eyes on him, their faces wily and in the know, without asking or wanting anything from him, as though they were observing a cloudy sky and waiting idly to see when the rain would start. So Larsen walked up to their table unbuttoning his coat, and growled: "Mind if I sit here?"

He skipped the starters to catch them up; they ate the soup, meat and the pudding together, talking all the while energetically, if insincerely, without taking sides, about the weather, crops, politics, the night life in the various provincial capitals. As they smoked over cups of coffee, Kunz, the older of the two, who seemed to have dyed hair and eyebrows, glanced at Galvez and questioned Larsen.

"So you are the new General Manager? How much? Three thousand? In any case, since Galvez here is head of administration, we'll know soon enough anyway. He has to register it in his books.

'Credited to señor Larsen' — it is Larsen, isn't it? — 'the sum of two or three or five thousand pesos, in payment of salary for the month of June.' "

Larsen looked them over at his leisure, first one and then the other; he had a resounding insult ready, ideally suited to his deep voice and laconic delivery. But he could not be sure they were making fun of him; Kunz, the older man, hairy, round-faced and plump, squat as a spider, the skin of his face creased by a few deep furrows, was staring at him with nothing more than curiosity and a gleam of childlike hope in his jet black eyes; the other one, Galvez, was showing his adolescent's teeth in a frank smile, while he calmly stroked his bald head.

They're amused, that's all, as if they're after some gossip they can tell tonight to the women they haven't got. Or perhaps they do, heaven help the four of them. There's no reason to start a fight.

"That's right, as you say," Larsen said. "I'm the Manager, or will be if sēnor Petrus accepts my conditions. And of course, it goes without saying, I have to study the company's real situation."

"Its real situation?" Galvez echoed him. "Of course."

"We have only just met," Kunz said, flashing a respectful smile. "But it's only fair to tell you the truth."

"Just a moment," Galvez cut in. "You're the technical expert. It's up to you to say if things are rotting from damp from the river, or are going rusty. Everything rots in the long run; everything gets rusted over and has to be thrown away or sold. That's your job, and to find new business: Technical Manager, two thousand pesos. I never forget, each month, to charge them to Jeremias Petrus Limited. But this is different, this is my affair. Señor Larsen, assuming you do decide to accept the post of General Manager, what wage do you have in mind, if I may ask? It's only out of curiosity, you understand. I'll write down whatever you say, a hundred or two million pesos, with all due respect."

"I know a thing or two about keeping accounts," Larsen said with a smile.

"You could give our friend some idea," Kunz said, also smiling, pouring himself wine. "You could betray your secrets and tell him what his predecessors used to get."

"Yes, I'd already decided that," Galvez agreed, nodding his bald head. "That's why I was asking. All I wanted to know was what señor Larsen considered a proper wage for the post of General Manager of the shipyard."

"You should tell him what the previous ones got."

"Thanks, but that doesn't interest me," Larsen said. "I've been thinking it over. I won't stay for less than five thousand. Five thousand a month and commission on future turnover." He raised the coffee cup to lick out the sugar, feeling out of place and ridiculous, but he could not stop himself, could not take a step back to avoid the trap. "I'm too old to prove myself. That's enough for me, that's what I could earn elsewhere. What interests me is getting the company going. I know there are millions around."

"What about it?" Kunz asked Galvez, craning forward across the tablecloth.

"That's fine," Galvez said. "Wait." He stroked his head, and leaned close to Larsen smiling "Five thousand. Congratulations. That's the top rate. I've had General Managers of two, three, four and five. That's the right rate for the job. But let me tell you: the last one who got paid five thousand, another German by the name of Schwartz, who borrowed a shotgun so he could kill me or the pioneer Petrus — it was never clear which — who stood guard for a week at the back door between my house and the office building, then finally took off, to the Chaco they say. Well, he worked for five thousand a year ago. Just to give you an idea. I know the currency has devalued since then. I think you could ask for six thousand, don't you agree, Kunz?"

"I think that's fair," Kunz said, running his hands through his bushy hair, sad and serious all of a sudden. "Six thousand pesos. Not too much, not too little. It's the proper rate for the job."

Then Larsen lit a cigarette and leaned back, smiling, forced to defend something he knew nothing about, despite feeling so ridiculous and out of place.

"Thanks again," he said. "Five thousand is fine. We'll start tomorrow. I warn you I like hard work."

The two men nodded, asked for more coffee, spent time and silence passing round cigarettes and matches. They stared at the grey muddy street outside the window: Galvez jerked his bald head back in anticipation of a sneeze that did not come, then called for the bill and signed it. The sun reflected in the furthest puddle of the street, a dirty dun colour. Larsen thought of Angelica Ines and Josefina, of things from the past he valued for the consolation they brought him.

"Have it your own way, five thousand it is," Galvez said, after glancing across at Kunz. "It's all the same to me, it's the same job. But they say — word gets around here — that you are almost the son-in-law. My congratulations if that's true. A nice girl plus the thirty million. Not hard cash, of course, and it won't all be yours; but nobody can tell me that isn't the value of the company's share capital."

Lost and beginning to realise it, provocative but lethargic, Larsen rolled his cigarette across his mouth with his lips.

"As far as that's concerned, nothing is definite, and anyway, it's a personal matter," he said slowly. "Don't get me wrong, all you two need know is that I am the General Manager and that tomorrow morning we start work in earnest. I'm going to spend this afternoon sending telegrams and talking on the phone to Buenos Aires. You can do what you like today. I'll be in the office at eight o'clock tomorrow morning, and then we can make a start on reorganising everything."

He stood up, listlessly put on his tight-fitting overcoat. He felt sad and irresolute, searching in vain for a way of taking leave of them that would bolster his position, knowing no other strategy than hate, behaving as if drunk and summoning impulses he no longer believed in.

"At nine," Galvez said, smiling up at him. "We never arrive before nine. But if you need me, run across to the cabin behind the shed, the hangar, and call me. At any time, I won't mind."

"Señor Larsen," Kunz got up, an expression of innocence on a face where the lines stood out like livid scars. "A pleasure to eat with you. It will be five thousand, as you request. But allow me to tell you you're not asking for much: next to nothing, in fact."

"See you tomorrow," Larsen said.

But all this happened twenty-four hours later, by which time it was too late. That midday when he met Petrus and took on the job of General Manager although he had not yet fixed his salary, Larsen forgot lunch and, after evoking the people, their concerns, the gestures that had vanished from the offices that once divided the huge room, he slowly and noisily made his way down the iron staircase which led to the sheds and what was left of the wharf.

He walked down awkwardly, feeling unreal and exposed, shuddering theatrically when the walls disappeared on the second flight and the grating iron steps plunged into the void. Then he crossed the dank sandy ground, protecting shoes and trousers from the thrusting weeds. He stopped beside a truck, its wheels stuck in the sand; only a few rusty parts remained under the open bonnet. He spat downwind at the truck. *I can't believe it. Doesn't the old man see these things? If they'd taken care of it, just by putting it under cover, it's worth fifty thousand at least.* He straightened up determinedly, walked past a wooden cabin with three worn steps up to its front door, then went into a huge doorless warehouse he eventually learnt to call the shed or hangar.

Despite the cold, the dim light, the wind moaning through the holes in the tin roof, despite feeling weak from hunger, Larsen strode, small and observant, along the rows of rusty, incomprehensible machines, the passageway between the enormous racks of shelving, their rectangular pigeonholes full of screws, bolts, clamps, nuts, drill bits, determined not to be put off by the desolation, the pointless division of space, the eyes of tools pierced by the nettles' spiteful stalks. He came to a halt at the far end of the shed, next to a pile of liferafts, *room for eight, canvas completely rotten, unperishable wood, rubber sides, a thousand pesos at the very least*, and picked up a blueprint with machinery and writing traced in white. It was stiff with mud, with long blades of grass stuck to it.

"What a way to let things go," he said out loud, full of bitter contempt. "If it's no use, it should be filed, not thrown away in the shed. Things'll have to change. The old man is crazy to put up with it."

He was not even talking to hear the sound of his own voice. The wind came spiralling gently down and wafted unhurriedly in through one side of the shed. All his words, the curses, threats, or gestures of defiance, were forgotten almost as soon as he uttered them. There was nothing more, from the beginning to the end of time, than the lofty ceiling above him, the flaking rust, tons of scrap metal, the weeds growing blindly, intertwining. Tolerated, a passer-by, an outsider, he too was there in the centre of the shed, powerless but absurdly mobile, like a black insect waving its legs and antennae in an air redolent of legend, of sea adventures, of past labours, of winter.

He stuffed the blueprint into his overcoat pocket, trying not to get dirty. One side of his mouth curled into a forgiving, manly smile — as if directed towards old rivals, defeated so often that their mutual antagonism had become as bland and comforting as a habit — at the desolation, the space, the ruin. He clasped his hands behind his back and spat a second time, at nothing in particular, but at everything, all that was visible or represented, all that came to mind without need of words or images; at fear, ignorance of every kind, at misery, devastation and death. He spat without moving his head, co-ordinating lips and tongue perfectly. He spat upwards and straight in front, expertly and conclusively, following the arc of the missile with abstract pleasure. He did not think of the word "office" or the word "desk", but said to himself: *I'm going to set myself up in the room with the switchboard, seeing that old man Petrus has kept the biggest room for himself, the one which has, still has, glass partitions.*

It must have been two in the afternoon. Galvez and Kunz had probably already returned to finish the stocktaking; it was too late to get a meal at Belgrano's. He pushed himself away from the heap of liferafts rotting beneath a hole in the roof, hands stuffed in his pockets, precisely aware of every inch of his height, the width of his shoulders, the pressure of his heels on the permanently damp earth, the tenacious patches of grass. He began to walk towards the shed door. As he went, hat negligently on the back of his head, his eyes flitted from side to side, dutifully distrustful, reviewing the rows of reddish machinery, silent perhaps forever, the monotonous geometrical shapes of the racks full of heaps of tools that stretched on and on, filthy and uninvolved, up to the ceiling beyond sight, beyond the top step of any conceivable ladder.

He proceeded slowly, at a pace he judged suited to this kind of ceremony, deliberately taking upon himself all the weight of bitterness and scepticism in defeat, drawing this feeling out of the metal objects in their tombs, the bulky machines in their mausoleums, the cenotaphs of weeds, mud and shadow, neglected corners that five or ten years earlier had been occupied by a workman's proud obstinacy, a foreman's vulgarity. Larsen went on, watchful, keen, implacable, paternal, secretly majestic, determined to hand out promotions and dismissals, needing to believe all this was his, needing to surrender himself wholeheartedly to it all with the sole aim of endowing it with meaning, and to bestow that meaning on the years he had left to live, and through them on the whole of his life. Step by step, treading the soft floor noiselessly, eyes flicking constantly to right and left, at ruined machinery, at pigeonholes blocked by cobwebs. Step by step until he emerged into the cold, feeble wind, into the damp air thickening into mist; already lost, already trapped.

The Summerhouse II

So Larsen was already under the spell, his fate decided, when he went into Belgrano's the next day to have lunch with Galvez and Kunz. It was never entirely clear whether he chose to head the monthly wages list with five or six thousand pesos. In fact, his choice of one or the other figure could only have mattered to Galvez, who typed out several copies on the 25th of each month, stopping every now and then to furiously rub his bald patch. Every 25th of the month, he once again discovered, was forced to recognise, the repeated, permanent absurdity he was in the grip of. This realisation made him break off, stand up, and pace about the huge deserted office, hands behind his back, his brown scarf wrapped round his neck, pausing at the drawing board where Kunz was always ready with his hollow, silent, exasperated laugh.

So it was either five or six thousand pesos that were punctually entered into the books, five or six depending on whether Larsen's superstitions leaned towards odd or even numbers. He had chosen that figure and all that went with it, so now each morning he got to the shipyard before anyone else, or so he liked to think while he sat there shivering, unable to admit it was only Galvez and Kunz he had beaten to the room now known as the General Manager's office, dominated by the telephone switchboard and its tangle of black cables, slightly less dusty and filthy nowadays, but irredeemably deaf and dumb.

That poor fat little man, that corpse without a tomb, that busy little ant, Larsen could have said of himself two months earlier if he had caught sight of this figure going into the General Manager's office at eight in the morning, taking off his hat, overcoat and gloves, lowering his body into the tattered leather chair, starting to go through the mound of files he had chosen and left on the desk the previous afternoon.

The buzzers worked, or rather were working again since he had spent a day fixing the wires. He had even painted the letters General Manager on the frosted glass of his partition door. In mid-morning he broke off from the tedium of the blue-papered "Dear Sirs", always headed with a date five or ten years earlier; broke off from the tales of prices, tonnage, experts' reports, offers and inevitable counter proposals, to press one of the two buzzers on his desk, Galvez or Kunz, to straighten his tie, try out a look and a smile to himself. As soon as they heard the agitated buzz, one or other of them began to chortle; they knocked at the door, they asked permission to enter, called him sir.

There was of course no question of him receiving either five or six thousand pesos at the end of any month. But nobody could deny him the satisfaction of offering a seat with a smile, a friendly gesture, to whichever of the two pushed open the glass door of his office, nor the ridiculous pleasure of asking questions and receiving answers about topics that sounded important but in all probability meant nothing at all: fluctuations in the balance of payments, current limits for compression in ships' boilers.

Larsen crossed his legs, pressed the tips of his fingers together before his mouth, his oval face all sceptical attention, and sometimes imagined he was Petrus himself, entrusted with his experiences and interests.

Every single lie, absurdity, or derisive joke that the person opposite him, Galvez or Kunz, invented with a profusion of smiles, nods, inappropriate "General Manager, sirs" — warmed Larsen's heart.

"I understand, of course, without a doubt, obviously, just as I thought," he would say during the pauses, as discreetly pleased as though he were lending a friend money.

Whenever he felt the boredom of midday approaching, he would tear a sheet from the desk diary that was years out of date and scribble down what struck him as the oddest things he had just heard. He would have liked to leap up and give Galvez or Kunz a big hug, to confess in an obscene phrase, to clap him on the back. Wistfully he restrained himself from thanking him, and dismissing him with a brief wave of the hand, adding only a friendly, encouraging smile.

He would wait until he heard them leave, then carefully tear up the pieces of paper covered with their strange, doubtful phrases; put on his coat, hat and gloves, and stare out of a glassless window at the desolation beyond: the big shed, the wasteland of puddles and weeds around it; then stride out, his shoes echoing on the dusty floor of the empty main office. He entered Belgrano's by the screen door, the one which led to the toilets and the hen coop; he would go up to his room and read *El Liberal* until lunch, shivering in the wicker armchair covered with threadbare cretonne, gesturing obscene defiance at the foretaste of winter pounding on the hotel roof. And in the afternoons, at the end of a day devoted to shifting, shaking and browsing through the files which recorded purchases and jobs that meant nothing to him despite all the best efforts of his imagination, that could no longer mean anything to anyone, Larsen made sure he was the last to leave the offices, turned the keys in useless locks, and went to Belgrano's to shave and put on his silk shirt, always gleaming white despite the frayed cuffs. If he bumped into the proprietor on the way out, he invented plausible destinations, then made lengthy detours along dirt roads and tracks, tracing ever varying and uncertain routes, twisting, novel paths born of deceit and duplicity.

Sooner or later he rang the heavy bell, passed through the iron gate, gave the maid (now mocking, sullen) a smile tinged with obviously repressed emotion, a tiny twist to his mouth, a look, all of which spoke of resignation and invited her to share it. Hatless, he followed her (though by now he needed no guide), through the perfumes and stems of the garden, between the walls of swift night pierced by the statues' unchanging whiteness.

Fifty metres from the gate, and his smile had lost all its melancholy: he was youth and its faith in life, he was the one who ploughs or conquers a future for himself, the one who builds a brighter tomorrow, the one who dreams and achieves, the immortal one. And perhaps before he sat on the handkerchief spread on the iron seat he kissed her, before he prolonged the smile which told of his delight and amazement: all day long I have sighed for this moment, and now I cannot believe it is true.

Or perhaps they only kissed after they had heard the maid and the dog's barks withdraw to the house on its concrete pillars, the house he, Larsen, could not enter. ("Just to see, to be in the rooms you live in, the dining-room, the hall, the sewing-room," he had asked. She blushed, crossed her legs; face to the ground, she laughed and then said no, never, not unless Petrus invited him.)

Or perhaps at that time they did not yet kiss. It is possible that Larsen was still cautious, waiting for the inevitable moment when he would discover what kind of woman Petrus' daughter was, which long forgotten Maria or Gladys she corresponded to, which technique of seduction he could employ to avoid any horror or hysteria, a premature end to the affair. "She's crazier than anyone I can remember," Larsen mused in his bed at Belgrano's, with a mixture of irritation and admiration. "All I know is she has breeding, she's the oddest person I've met, she's never had a man."

If this was the case, if fear of failure and something more that

Larsen could not explain prevailed over his sense of the duty or professional pride that was driving him to possess her as soon as possible, to waste no time in setting up the only base from which he could make sense of his relations with women, it is legitimate to admit, as the most important and fruitful version of their twilight meetings in the summerhouse, the one Angelica Ines would have given, had she been capable of forming a complete sentence:

"I start to perspire, to pace up and down, two hours, one hour before he arrives. Because I'm afraid, and just as afraid he might not come. I put on cream and perfume. I stare at his mouth when he hitches up his trousers to sit down; when I laugh I hide my face behind my hands so I can look at him as long as I like, without feeling embarrassed. In the summerhouse, he takes my hand; he smells of bay rum, of me, of when daddy used to smoke cigars in the bathroom, of dried soapsuds. I may feel sick, but not disgusted. Josefina, la Negra, just laughs; she knows everything but won't say a word; yet she doesn't know what I know. I coax her, give her presents so that she'll ask me. But she has never asked me that, because she doesn't know about it, or can't imagine it. When she's annoyed, she laughs, asks me things I don't want to understand. Cream and perfume; I look out of the window or give Dick a kiss. Dick barks, wants to go out, wants me to go with him. I think true things and made-up ones, sometimes I get confused between them, I always know when it's time, I'm hardly ever wrong, he has no choice but to arrive just as I'm saying: 'he's walking from the corner to the garden gate.'

"At first I would have liked him to be daddy's brother, and for his mouth, his hands, his voice·to change with the time of day. Only those things. He comes, he loves me; he must want to come, I didn't go looking for him. They are friends now, they're always together in the office when I can't see them. Daddy stares up at the sky, his face thin and pale. Not like him. I go out and wait for him, I start laughing with Dick or at everything I come across, but only for a moment, so that I'm not laughing any more, or only in the way I want to, when he arrives, gives me his hand and starts staring at me. Then I laugh again, as I watch how he sits down: he takes his trouser legs between his fingers, hitches them both, then sits with his legs apart. It's at night that I think of true things, when he has gone and we light candles to the saints and the dead souls. But in the summerhouse I only think of lies; he talks to me, I stare at his mouth, give him my hand; he explains patiently who I am and what I'm like. But I cry as well. When I'm in bed it's the lies I remember, I see myself stroking the grass on the floor of the summerhouse with my shoes; I never hurt his feelings, I try to get to know him . I think of mummy, of the endless winter nights, of Lord sleeping standing up with the rain streaming off his back, I think of Larsen dead in a far-off place, I think and think and I cry."

THE CABIN I

The scandal must have happened sometime later. But perhaps it would be convenient to bring it up now so that it can be kept in mind. It must in any case have occurred before Larsen was once again staring misery in the face, before Poetters, the owner of Belgrano's, had stopped smiling and barely greeted him, before Larsen's credit for meals and laundry ran out. Before Larsen, heavy, irritated, lacking imagination — as in the days when he allowed himself to be called The Bodysnatcher — found himself reliving scenes from twenty or thirty years earlier: a diet of maté and tobacco, promises repeatedly given and never kept, humiliating bribes for the boy to supply him with an iron, a cigarette, hot water in the morning.

The scandal can be put off indefinitely; it may even be possible to suppress it. We might choose instead any moment before that afternoon when it seems Angelica Ines Petrus went into Larsen's office and as she came out again halted in the doorway between the general office and the main staircase, the wind swirling lazily around her, and slowly turned round, with no false pride or modesty, her coat unfastened, her dress torn from her breast, ripped down to the waist by her own hand, then went back towards GENERAL MANAGER'S OFFICE, painted in black on the grimy glass door.

We might for example prefer the moment when Larsen felt crushed by hunger and misfortune, cut off from life, lacking the heart to keep on inventing enthusiasms. One Saturday afternoon he was in his office reading an estimate for repairs written on the 23 February seven years earlier to Messrs Kaye & Son Co. Ltd., owners of the ship *Tiba*, then laid up in El Rosario. The wind and rain had not stopped for forty-eight hours. The dark, swollen river was ever present, unforgettable; for the past four or five days all Larsen had eaten were the cakes and biscuits he was offered with tea in the summerhouse.

He abandoned the file and slowly raised his head. He could hear the wind, the absence of noise from Galvez and Kunz. He also felt he could hear his hunger, which had shifted from his stomach to his head and his bones. Perhaps that March seven years before, the *Tiba* had sunk as she left El Rosario, laden with wheat. Perhaps her captain J. Chadwick had been able to sail her uneventfully back to London, where Kaye & Son Co. Ltd., (Houston Line) had had the repair work done on the Thames. Perhaps Kaye & Son, or Mr Chadwick acting on their behalf, had accepted the estimate, or a compromise price reached after bargaining, and the dirty grey unladen ship with its woman's name had come down river and anchored opposite the shipyard. But the truth was not to be found in that slender file containing no more than a press cutting, a letter from El Rosario, a copy of another letter signed by Jeremias Petrus, and the detailed estimate. The continuation of the *Tiba's* story, its happy or sad ending, must be lost somewhere in the heaps of files and folders that took up half a metre of Larsen's office wall and were scattered through the rest of the building. Perhaps he would find it on Monday, perhaps never. At any rate, he had hundreds of similar transactions at his disposal, with or without an ending; months, even years, of pointless reading in front of him.

He closed the file, scrawled his initials on the cover to show he had read it. He put on his coat, scooped up his hat, and went round locking all the doors and furniture in the offices, all those which worked, which had keys and bolts.

He came to a halt in the middle of the room which had once held Administration, the Typing Pool, part of the Technical Department and Exports. He stood by Galvez's desk, staring at the huge cloth-bound account books with Petrus' name on the front and index letters down the spine.

His hunger was not so much a desire to eat as a sadness at being alone and hungry, a feeling of nostalgia for a freshly laundered white tablecloth with tiny darns and stains from recent meals; for the sound of bread being broken, steaming plates, the cheerful vulgarity of companions.

He remembered the wooden cabin where Galvez lived, perhaps with a wife and children, down between the main shed and the reed beds. It was almost one o'clock. *This* Tiba *affair, these English people Chadwick & Son. When things like that happen, when we get to hear of them . . . does the firm simply send a letter, or do we employ an agent in El Rosario? I say El Rosario, but I mean any port that comes within our range. I'm sorry to bother you outside office hours.*

They did not let him say any of this. They took away his need to ask questions and lie the very moment he stopped, smiling and removing his hat in front of the squatting group, his body twisted slightly to prevent the smoke from the grill spoiling his overcoat. Without a word, without even looking at each other, they decided not to let him speak before they even saw him set foot in the windswept waste ground, as his short dark clumsy figure carefully placed one shiny shoe after another on the iron steps down, clutching his hat brim as though it were a weapon, a symbol of nobility, a precious offering.

"Would you like a maté? This is my wife. Excuse me while I see to the fire, it keeps trying to go out," Galvez said, smiling up out of swirling smoke and the sizzling meat.

Kunz had stood up and nodded a greeting; then he held out his hand and offered him a maté.

"Thanks; I only came by for a moment," Larsen said.

He took his hat off and stood with hand outstretched towards the beautiful, pregnant woman with dishevelled hair who was coming down the cabin steps, from where the planks surrounded the wooden building and which in all likelihood they called the porch, where they would sit on summer evenings to get fresh air from the river, maybe happy, maybe thankful. The woman was wearing a man's overcoat and shoes. Her bulky white figure swayed towards him. She was pushing back her hair, not in any attempt to tidy it or to apologise because it was uncombed and had become a mess, but simply to stop the wind blowing it into her eyes.

"This is an honour for me, señora," Larsen declared, in a swift clear tone, realising that the smile he had used in his past life whenever he first met a woman (a smile that was somehow knowing while being dazzled, protective, and provocative) had appeared effortlessly, unchanged by time or circumstances.

He began to drink the maté and glanced around him at the wooden house. It looked like an enlarged version of a dog kennel, with three broken steps leading up to the door, faint traces of blue paint, the wheelhouse from a barge, from the corpse of some *Tiba* or other, propped along one side.

He took in the suspicious pet dogs, the grey hump of the office building, the brick shed, heaps of corrugated iron, scrap metal, decay, the flat sheet of the river, unruffled by the wind.

"It's not bad here," he said with another easy, politely envious smile.

The woman, tall, unresponsive and with the dogs sheltered between her legs, shrugged her shoulders under the coat, and showed him her stained, childish teeth.

"He's come to see how the poor live," Galvez said, standing there with the maté gourd hiding his furious smile.

"I've come to see my friends," Larsen said gently, as if he had suddenly woken to the fact that the other man might mean it. The hot, bitter maté water ran through his innards. He sensed how easy it would be to start a fight, kick over the grill, stare at the woman, utter some obscenity.

"I was about to leave my office," he recited, examining his fingernails, "when it occurred to me to work on a report this weekend. I spent the morning going through the files. I came across an estimate sent several years ago to the captain of a ship that needed repairs in the port of El Rosario."

It occurred to him they were letting him go on talking out of malice, that they were adopting the sarcastic imitation of a respectful silence to force him to confess it was all a desperate farce. He pushed his hands in his pockets and stared down at the tips of his shoes which squelched in the scorched weeds, bits of paper stiff with mud, filthy puddles. On the porch the radio began to play a tango (later on he learnt that they called the planks sticking out from the side of the cabin their verandah), or perhaps it was now that he heard it for the first time.

"It concerns a ship, the *Tiba*, taking on wheat in El Rosario and needing repairs before it could set sail. There's no trace of what happened next. It'll be hard to find the rest of the file given the mess all the records are in," he was trying to find a way to leave: "in my opinion, one of our first measures will have to be to reorganise all the files and all our business records." He had accepted he must go mad or die, as in a detached way he observed his shoes moving in the rain-darkened earth, addressing his speech for no particular reason to the broad, immobile woman. When he could stand it no longer, he raised his head and looked at them one by one, the men, the woman, the dogs; hands in his pockets, breathing hard, his hat tilted over one ear, his eyes bright again, inquisitive.

"It depends on the year," Kunz said wistfully. "I don't remember dealing with that estimate."

Crouched down, Galvez was still gazing at the fire.

"Is it nearly ready?" the woman asked.

Galvez straightened up, knife in hand. He stared at her in surprise, as if unable to understand, as if her face or the question she had asked revealed something he was ashamed not to have noticed before. He smiled at her, kissed her on the forehead.

"The maté water's gone cold," Kunz continued. "If you show me the file on Monday, I might recognise it."

Galvez came over to Larsen, trying not to smile.

"Why don't you leave your coat inside?" he ordered gently. "And while you're at it, bring yourself a plate and a knife and fork. You'll see where they are. We're just about to eat."

Without looking at him, Larsen climbed the three steps, dropped his coat on the bed, put his hat back on, got a tin plate and a metal knife and fork, smiled generously at the three of them crouched in silence outside as if it were he who had bought all the food, then settled to watch the meat crackling as he sang to himself the words of regret and revenge that came from the nasal tango on the radio.

Then, slowly and cautiously, Larsen began to accept the possibility of combining the illusory management of Petrus Ltd., with other illusions, other kinds of lies he had sworn never to hide behind again.

Perhaps this had become inevitable when he realised in his heart of hearts that he would not collect his five or six thousand pesos at the end of this month or of any others he still had left to live; or when the proprietor at Belgrano's carried on reading the newspaper or swatting flies when Larsen came up to the bar with the smile of a loquacious drinker; or when he had to hide his shirt cuffs before he set off through the familiar maze of frozen statues that led to the summerhouse. Or perhaps he had simply let himself go, as at times of crisis one returns to the safe haven of a mania, a vice, a woman.

But this was the last chance he had to keep up the delusion. So, concealing his effort but with desperate determination, he maintained an impassable boundary between the General Manager's Office, the increasing cold of the summerhouse, and the meals in or outside the cabin where Galvez lived with the woman in her men's clothing and the filthy dogs.

Apart from occasional feelings of compassion and the awareness that he would never understand the secret behind the woman's constant cheerfulness (*It's not that she is resigned to her fate, it's not because of the privilege of sleeping with that fellow, but it's not because she's completely dumb either*) Larsen had little to put up with. In fact it was not them he was with, but with copies, more or less accurate, of other Galvez and Kunzes, other happy, miserable women, friends whose names and faces had been forgotten but who had helped him — without meaning to, without really taking him into account, without adding anything to the natural impulse of helping themselves — to make this feeling of being at bay, of utter despair, seem both normal and infinitely tolerable. For their part, from the very first day they accepted Larsen's double game without any sense of shame or mockery: his presence in the General Manager's office from 8 to 12 and 3 to 6, then his disappearance until dinner-time, his silences whenever they talked of old man Petrus, or made insinuations about his daughter's existence.

Those dinners (almost always some kind of stew these days, because the cold forced them to cook inside the cabin, and the smoke would have been a problem) went on a long while, with litres of wine, muffled tangos on the radio (the dogs would be asleep, the woman singing softly, tunelessly into the warmth of her raised lapels, smiling as each word she sang renewed the mystery of her happiness and intact innocence) with the relaxed exchange of anecdotes, colourful memories deliberately kept impersonal.

They no longer loathed Larsen, and it is almost certain that they accepted him because they thought he was mad, because he touched a corresponding layer of madness within themselves; because to hear his drawling voice talking of the price per metre for painting a ship's hull in 1947, or suggesting childish ways of making a lot more money out of careening phantom ships which would never come up river, offered them some obscure compensation; because they were entertained by the ups and downs of Larsen's struggle with poverty, his triumphs and failures in the endless, confused fight to display starched white collars, trousers with no sheen, properly laundered handkerchiefs, to put on faces, smiles and gestures that would clearly show the confidence, peace of mind, the insulting smugness that only wealth can bestow.

THE SUMMERHOUSE III
THE CABIN II

During those days, Larsen went down to Mercedes, two ports further south, to sell all he had left: a diamond and ruby brooch, a memento from a woman he could no longer place, the value of which he had watched increase with pleasure as the years went by.

He let himself be robbed blind, leaning nonchalantly against the counter. Then superstition drove him to another tiny jeweller's, as a sop to his determination, his memory: the shop was close to the market, opposite empty lots, and also sold silks and stockings, magazines, women's shoes. Separated by the narrow glass counter from an impassive moustachioed Turk, Larsen gave in to his old delight in caressing gifts for women, objects either useless or whose use was subtle, complicated; objects that struck up a rapid friendship with any hands or eyes that touched them, that went through the years slowly wearing out, docilely changing their meaning.

"Everything expensive, nothing worthwhile," he said to no avail, the words lost on the shopkeeper's sad, stubborn silence.

Eventually he gave in, and chose a gilt compact with a mirror, a crest on the lid, a powder puff he dabbed saucily on his nose and cheeks. He bought two the same.

"Wrap them up so they don't get scratched."

He ate lunch on his own in an unfamiliar restaurant, filled his pockets with bars of chocolate, and went back on the first ferry.

That night in Galvez's cabin they joked about his absence. Larsen ate with the proprietor of the Belgrano after he had settled his debt and paid him two months' rent on his room. He sat until dawn getting secretly drunk with him, talking about the watch industry, life's ups and downs, the boundless possibilities of a young country; towards the end, back again at the bar, he let slip that the Creditors Committee would release Petrus' thirty million at any moment, and that this was all he was waiting for to announce his engagement to Angelica Ines.

As he went up to bed, he remembered he still had two hundred pesos or so to put towards the meals at Galvez's. He fell asleep thinking he had reached the end, that in a couple of months he would have no bed, nothing to eat; that old age could not be concealed and that he no longer cared; that selling the brooch would bring him bad luck.

Then, after a confused early morning dream which it did not really interrupt, there came a day of work, begun in his office punctually at eight or nine with a resigned shake of the head at the heap of files about events dead and gone that he had put aside the day before. He read until he was distracted by the desire to go into the main office to join Kunz and Galvez at the empty table where they heated their eleven o'clock coffee. He had been hearing their movements and chat for some time. Galvez was bent over his account books, while the German was head down in the fresh blues of his plans, surrounded by the harsh, secret, disconnected figures on his pages of calculations.

An offer for asphalting machines and dump trucks helped him forget the two of them for a while, but they gradually crept back into his mind, and he slowly pushed back the file he was reading. He lit a cigarette, trying to move as little as possible. He could hear voices raised without enthusiasm, laughter with no response; the wind, boards creaking, a dog's bark, tiny points of sound that helped measure the distance and silence.

They're as crazy as I am, Larsen thought. He had thrust his head back and held it still in the cold air, eyes bulging, contempt showing on his pinched mouth as he screwed it up to support the cigarette. It was as if he were spying on himself, as if looking at himself from afar, from many years before, watching this fat, obsessed man spending the morning in a ruined, unlikely office, playing at reading critical reports of shipwrecks averted, of millions to be made. It was as though his old self of thirty years earlier were describing him as he was now, to his women and friends, in a world which they knew (he and the young men with their cheeks dusted with talc, he and the young women with their easy laughter) would be unchanging, suspended for ever in the enjoyment of promises, wealth, every kind of perfection; as if he were inventing an impossible Larsen, that he would point an accusing finger at the aberration.

For a few seconds, he could see himself at a unique point in time; at a specific age, in a determined place, with a past. It was as though he had just died, as if the rest could no longer be anything more than an act of memory, experience, calculation, idle curiosity.

"And they're just as farcical as I am. They couldn't give a damn about Petrus, me or the thirty millions; they don't even believe that this is or has been a shipyard; they sit politely while the old man, me, the flies, the building and the river itself tell them tales of ships which came here, of two hundred workmen, of shareholders' meetings, of debentures and shares which rose and fell on the stock market. They don't even believe in what they actually touch and do, in the figures they write down, about money, weight and size. But they climb the iron staircase every day, they come to play at seven hours' work and feel that the game is somehow more real than the spiders, the leaky pipes, the rats, the spongy, rotten wood. And if they are mad, I must be crazy too. Because I could play my game all on my own, whereas if they, others, join in, it's the game that counts, it becomes the real thing. To accept that, for me, who was playing it merely as a game, is to accept madness."

He was wide awake, tired, weak. He spat out the cigarette, stood up, pushed open the door of the General Manager's Office. Smiling and rubbing his hands together, he went over to the table where Galvez and Kunz sat, swinging their legs to and fro while they drank coffee.

"Is there a shot for me?" Larsen asked, before pouring himself some. "A coffee to finish off a meal, a coffee to finish off hunger. It's better than any aperitif. It's a shame all those kilometres of railway line were never used. The idea of a highway alongside was good, but then of course they had to obtain the concession."

"Well, at least there are the sleepers," Galvez said. "We burn them for cooking and heating."

"Not everything goes to waste," the German said consolingly.

"It's still a shame," Larsen said. He put the cup down on the table, stared at the other two, dabbed his lips with a handkerchief. "I won't be in my office this afternoon. I'll leave fifty pesos for this evening, so you can buy things and we can celebrate."

"But it isn't Saturday today," Kunz said.

"Never mind," Galvez said; "We'll enjoy ourselves. There's no point worrying; the accounts are well in the black."

After lunch, Larsen stretched out on the bed and in his sleep dreamt of concave walls made up of familiar faces, looking down at him with chaste expressions of puzzlement and disapproval. He woke up to find himself (cold, dyspeptic, still in his waistcoat) flat on his back in bed, listening to the first signs of day's end in the cries of remote animals, and the sound of the proprietor's voice underneath his window. He felt for a cigarette, stretched a blanket over his feet, stared at the fading light on the ceiling, and imagined a country childhood, shared by all mankind, a paradise that was wintry, calm, maternal. Beyond the cigarette smoke he smelt a whiff of ammonia, a beach abandoned by fishermen. Once a week a pipe burst or a latrine overflowed. The proprietor stood outside in rubber boots giving orders to the two maids and the boy.

Larsen waited until the sun's rays on the ceiling told him it was six o'clock. Facing the mirror, he stroked the stubbly flesh on his chin, slicked his hair back with water, poured talc on three fingers and rubbed it into his cheeks, forehead and nose. He refused to think while he was tying his tie, putting his coat on, choosing one of the compacts. *This fellow staring at me in the mirror.* He walked stiffly out into the still, cold evening air, along the sodden earth road which swallowed the sound of his heavy footsteps, his dark figure dwarfed beneath the lofty trees.

The gate was shut. He looked up at the pale lights in the windows, listened to the silence with a dog at its centre, pulled three times on the bell cord. *I could shoot myself*, he thought glumly, sorry for himself. The dog had fallen silent; someone broke away from the first deep blue shadow of night, skirted the summerhouse and walked towards him along the brick path. The dog was loping along, panting; it barked at the gate, the statues, to right and left. The light was fading from the treetops. *I could also* . . . Larsen thought, then shrugged, clasping the compact in his pocket.

It was not Josefina but Angelica Ines who was making her way in stops and starts towards him, dressed in a long white dress with a narrow waist, the dog bounding round her.

"I had given you up," she said. "Daddy's arriving at any moment, so we locked the gate because he doesn't like it open. Josefina is at work in the kitchen."

"I had a lot to do," Larsen explained. "A lot of work, and a trip to Santa Maria to get something. Guess what."

She finally managed to open the gate and pushed the dog back. She laughed as she pretended to search for a stone to scare off the animal, then laughed with face upturned as she gave Larsen her arm. A perfume of summer flowers enveloped her. As they walked towards the summerhouse, he could see a yellow light inside, a steady glow that deepened as the night and their footsteps advanced.

They entered the candles' scarcely troubled gleam. Larsen noted the heavy candelabra with suspicion — it was ancient, tarnished, with the shapes of animals and flowers — standing weightily in the centre of the stone table. *It looks like something Jewish, it looks all silver.*

Leaning on the table, she laughed again, and this time the flames flickered. Her white dress reached down to the shiny ribbons on her shoes, the candlelight shone on the imitation pearls that hung from her neck and bodice. Larsen respectfully took his hat off, and stood sniffing at the damp and the cold, contrasting them with the whiteness of her dress.

"I've taken the liberty of bringing you a keepsake," he said, stepping forward to show her the compact. "I's not much, but perhaps you'll appreciate the thought."

Square, brand new, aggressive, the compact burnished the flames from the candles. The woman laughed again, like a bird's trill, demurred but stretched out her arms in excited disbelief until she snatched the little metal container. The dog was running to and fro in the distance, barking; the sky suddenly turned completely dark and the flames burned higher, more intensely, as if with a vengeful joy.

"Something to remember me by," Larsen said, going no closer to her. "So that you can open it and see those eyes, that mouth of yours. So that you understand, looking at yourself, that it is impossible to live without you."

His voice had sounded convincing, choked with emotion and respect. As she looked at her parted lips in the mirror, moving her head, her clenched teeth, from side to side, she was probably picturing a night without Larsen, a night with Larsen gone forever. But he felt a fool at his own attitude, at the distance between them, at his bent knee, the hat clutched across his stomach; he was painfully aware of his clumsiness, the failure of his gestures, yet full of admiration at the preciseness of the words he had just uttered.

"It's pretty, it's so pretty." She pressed the compact against her bosom as though protecting it from the cold, looked defiantly at Larsen. "It's mine now."

"Yes, it's yours," Larsen said, "to remember me by." He could not think of any beautiful or fitting words to add, and accepted that the story should end with this encounter between her and the gilt box, at the start of a winter's evening, by the light of seven candles burning down in the cold air. He left his hat on the table, went over to her, a sad, beseeching smile on his face.

"If you only knew . . ." he began uncertainly. She drew back, swaying away from him, her shoulders hunched to protect the compact.

"No," she cried, then began to murmur in a sing-song, spellbound voice: "No, no, no . . ." but as soon as Larsen touched her shoulders, she relaxed her hold on the gift and offered him her mouth. Her head level with the base of the candelabra, she laughed, cried without protest. When finally they stood upright again, they were assailed by footsteps and cries from Josefina, by the bounding, panting dog.

She rolled her eyes and tried to produce more tears; her sleeve caught the flame and Larsen smothered it with his hand. There was a smell of singed hair as he felt for the compact on the floor.

Josefina was close by in the darkness, promising the dog a treat. Larsen picked up his hat, kissed Angelica Ines on the forehead.

"Never in my wildest dreams," he lied fervently.

As he was approaching the cabin that night, head sunk deep inside his coat and scarf for warmth, he found it impossible to rejoice in his victory, or even to be able to see it as one. He felt diminished, incapable of boasting, incredulous as though it were not true that he had kissed Angelica Ines in the candles' golden, quivering diamonds, or that she was not really a woman, or it had not been he who had done it.

For many years, the conquest of a woman had been for him no more than an unavoidable rite, a task to be performed efficiently, expeditiously, in spite of or aside from the pleasure received. He had done it, time and again, without concern or problems, like a boss paying a wage; carrying out his duty, confirming the other's submission. But even in the saddest, most forced cases he had extracted from love a sense of fullness, a misplaced pride, even on those occasions when he had to exaggerate his cynicism and the twisted curl of his smile in response to silent friends who during reunions prolonged till dawn yawned sleeplessly when they saw Larsen's woman finally arrive. They would struggle to break the silence, coming out with the first heroic phrase they could concoct or recall: "Labruna is doubtful for the game."

Not now; now there was no room for pride or a sense of shame. He was empty, cut off from his memory. He spat noisily when the brick wall at the back of the shipyard came to an end on his left; he could see the warm light of the fire and its reflection on the shed's tin roof. He spat again as he turned towards the cabin, as he composed himself, as a murmur of music, branches burning and the smell of meat grilling was carried to him on the freezing, calm wind.

"Women are all mad," he thought, cheering himself up.

He groped forward numbly, feeling for the curving brick path in the mud. His head was up, an expression of joy and kindness spreading across his face as he emerged out of the darkness into the firelight. He was nearing the party that he himself had paid for.

"Good evening one and all," he shouted when they caught sight of him. He crossed their greetings and stroked the dogs' muzzles.

After the meal he was alone for a moment in the cabin with the woman. His face when he gave her the compact wore the same nostalgic, contrite look as when he had stroked the dogs. All he said was:

"Something to remember me by, to open and look at yourself in."

The woman — sullen, unkempt and grimy, her man's overcoat closed under her chin with an enormous safety pin, made shapeless by her swollen belly, the greasy shine of her face circumscribing a knowledge it was pointless if not impossible to transmit — protested feebly, smiled sardonically, looked at Larsen with indulgent affection, as if he were her father or her elder brother, someone tolerated because he was good at heart despite being so odd.

"Thank you, it's pretty," she said. She opened it and moved her snub nose from side to side in the mirror. "I've no idea what good it is to me . . . it's ridiculous of you to buy it for me. But you did right, it doesn't matter. If you had asked me, I'd have said I didn't want anything, but I'd have been thinking of a compact just like this one." She closed it, to enjoy hearing the noise of its spring by her ear. She tilted it so that the gilt and the heart-shaped crest caught the light, then put it in her pocket. "The water must be ready for coffee. What would you like? Would you like me to give you a kiss?"

She offered this openly, with no hint of malice. Larsen lit a cigarette, smiled at her, overwhelmed. For a second he toyed with the desperate, faint hope: *She's a real woman. If only she were to take a bath, put on a proper dress, make-up. If only I had met her a few years ago.* He added to his ecstasy a touch of melancholy.

"No, thanks señora I don't want anything."

"Well then go outside and talk with the others. I'll bring out the coffee."

He shrugged and left the cabin without looking back. For the second time that night, he took out with him into the cold air a feeling that he had won an intricate, useless victory. They drank their coffee by the fire, went on pouring wine from the demijohn and discussing politics, football, other people's business successes. The woman was already asleep with the dogs inside the cabin when Galvez stirred, smiled at Larsen.

"You may not believe it," he said, darting a glance at Kunz. "But I can send old man Petrus to jail whenever I choose."

Larsen bent to light his cigarette from a burning ember. He asked casually: "Why would you want to do that? Even if you could, where would it get you?"

"There are reasons," Kunz murmured. "It's a long story."

Seated on his box, the cigarette slanting across his face, Larsen waited. Kunz coughed. One of the dogs came running out, licked the fat around the grill, cautiously cracked a bone. A cock crowed in the distance, and night closed in around them. Out of the corner of his eye, Larsen saw the curve of Galvez's broad blank smile directed to the heavens.

"You don't believe me," Galvez said, a note of sadness in his voice. *It's not a smile, he's neither happy nor sarcastic, he was born like that, with his lips parted and his teeth clenched.* "But I can."

Larsen tried in vain to recall when, where and in whom he had heard that note of impure hatred, of calm self-assuredness before. It must have been the voice of a woman, threatening him or one of his friends with dire consequences in some distant future.

Galvez was still smiling, head tilted back. Larsen spat out his cigarette, and the three of them sat staring out into the black winter's night, at the path reflected like silver filings, at the persistence of the scattered stars calling out to be named.

THE SHIPYARD III
THE CABIN III

At ten o'clock the next morning, Kunz knocked on the General Manager's door. He came in, grinning sheepishly, exposing a gold tooth to the light. (The light was grey, lifeless, a light that arrived defeated after its struggle through giant clouds of water and cold. The weather had broken, an indifferent wind came whistling through all the holes in the building.)

Larsen lifted his head from the piles of folders and sniffed, uncaring, at the mockery, the game, the hidden despair.

"Excuse me," Kunz said, bowing and clicking one worn-down heel against the other. "The Administrative Manager requests an appointment with the General Manager. The favour of an appointment. The Administrative Manager considers himself in a position to document, in every sense of the word, the truth of certain verbal allegations."

Larsen stared at him, mouth and shoulders twitching. Silence, bitterness, desolation. Plumped on top of the double fold of a faded red scarf, the man's head seemed neither drunk nor belligerent. It was more that this kind of convoluted message was completely out of character; nothing could have been sadder than the unmoving darkness of his eyes.

"Have him come in," Larsen said, flashing his teeth in a dazzling smile. "My office is always open."

The German nodded silently, turned on his heel, and went out. Still playing the game, tense with expectation, energy, cruelty, almost young again, Larsen took his revolver from under his arm and put it in the half-open drawer that pressed against his stomach. The wind was stirring the papers on the floor, swirling around the high ceilings. Galvez knocked at the door, brought his set smile (with no hint of challenge) up to the desk. His cheek bones stood out, older, yellower.

"The Technical Manager has informed me ..." Larsen started to say in measured tones, but the man in front of him held up his hand, broadened his smile, gently placed on the table, like the clinching card of a victory he regretted, a tattered piece of green cardboard.

Taken aback, Larsen examined the whirling scrolls round the edges, then read: Jeremias Petrus Ltd., authorised issue, ten thousand pesos, chairman, secretary, shares issued to the bearer.

"So you have a certificate for ten thousand pesos."

"Strange, isn't it? Ten thousand pesos. Remember last night I told you I could send him to jail."

Now a sound was added to the smile, a tiny explosion like a cockroach being squashed.

"Yes," Larsen said.

"Understand?"

"Understand what?"

"The certificate is a forgery. He forged it: this one and I don't know how many more. This one is forged anyway, and he signed it. Look: J. Petrus. There were two genuine share issues, the one founding the company, then another to enlarge the capital. This certificate doesn't belong to either issue. And he signed it. He sold a lot of these."

The finger jabbing at the signature was the colour of rancid cheese. The hand scooped the card from the desk.

"Well," Larsen said, content, at ease. "You must be sure about this, you know these things. So he forged certificates. Old man Petrus. You can send him to jail, and as far as I can tell he'll stay there for a good few years."

"For this?" Galvez laughed again, tapping the pocket where he had put the certificate away. "He'll never get out. He won't live long enough to complete his sentence."

"It's disgraceful," Larsen said, staring at a window. "We ought to sell something to buy new glass and cover the holes."

"Yes, it's not exactly pleasant in winter." Galvez's smile faltered, became limp. He looked out at the rainy morning. "We sell off two thousand pesos' worth of goods from the sheds each month. Kunz and me: fifty-fifty. The German didn't have the nerve to ask you to join in; I don't want you to think we didn't tell you so we could keep it for ourselves."

"What else could we do?" he was still staring at the triangular hole in the window-pane, gaunt, old-looking, the corners of his mouth still quivering. "It could just as easily be three thousand. There's probably enough for a year or two."

Larsen had wondered how they managed to live.

"My thanks," he said. "OK, it's true, you can send him to jail, but where would that get us?"

"Nowhere," Galvez replied. "If he's put away, we'd lose everything. They'd kick us out in twenty-four hours. It's not that. It's just because that old bastard deserves to end his days in jail. You've no idea."

"No," Larsen agreed, thoughtful. "I haven't. Perhaps it's better, perhaps not. Do whatever you like."

"Thanks," Galvez said, his smile broad and taut once more. "Thanks for giving me permission."

Carefully, with disgust, sadly, as if afraid of cutting himself on it, Larsen put the gun back in his shoulder holster, then slumped back in his seat. The wind was blowing drops of freezing drizzle in through the broken windows. They bounced with a fleeting gaiety on the flimsy sheets of a report on metallisation that lay strewn over the desk.

Doubting, puffing his lips out and making a sound like humming telegraph wires, Larsen screwed up his eyes to see how far away he could read. "Shipbuilders and naval repair yards have been greatly assisted in overcoming a host of problems thanks to metallisation. However high quality and rust-resistant paints may be, they do not protect steel or iron from the electro-chemical reaction which takes place whenever they come into contact with oxygen. Zinc is the only effective anti-corrosive on iron or steel, since it closes the electrogalvanic circuit, thereby avoiding any electro-chemical reaction."

Larsen was not worried that life was slipping by, dragging the things that mattered to him away into the distance. He was suffering, his mouth agape, a cold bubble of saliva on his lips, aware of the fat his chin was sinking into, because those things no longer really interested him, because he no longer wanted them instinctively, not enough to sustain them or to give purpose to his guile. *There's at least a thousand pesos a month, even before I take a hand and show those lads how we can make more without ruining ourselves, without using up our capital. There's no problem. Yet when I'm told the story of those forged certificates, when I hear this character's been sleeping for heaven knows how long with the evidence stuffed inside his vest, like a kid with a loaded pistol, it leaves me cold, I don't do anything, I don't have a single idea, I really don't know what to choose for the best.*

Larsen craned forward, impassive, almost innocent, revelling in this lonely doublecross, somehow suspecting that the deliberate game of going on being Larsen was infinitely more childish than the one he was now playing. Pressing against the desk, his eyes almost closed, he read with his arms at full stretch: "According to your requirements, we can furnish the widest range of materials, from high-carbon steels, stainless steels, to bronze, phosphorus and Babbit anti-friction metal."

A few raindrops splashed his cheek. He stood up and listened to the silence that lay beneath the wind. He gathered up the sheets of the report, humming three isolated verses of a tango to himself, repeating them over and over with a calm, jubilant rage. When he reached the door, he tipped his hat to one side, and thought he had forgotten something: he felt like laughing, like testing the closeness of a true friend, like committing an act of cruelty which no one would be able to explain.

At noon he swaggered, stiff-legged, overcoat undone, into the huge, deserted office. He stared at Galvez and Kunz's tables, at the desks that had not yet been used for firewood, at the dented filing cabinets, the discarded, useless, incomprehensible typewriters. The wind was fluttering among the yellowing newspapers that had protected the floor from the leaky roof; outside, a stream of water dripped from a broken pipe into tin cans. Larsen buttoned his coat, almost happy, on the move again, a barely hidden, vengeful grin on his face, while he imagined the bustling noise in the office five or ten years earlier.

He went down the iron staircase in the drizzle, made his way across the mud without anyone in the cabin spotting him. He went at a run, as if he were seeing everything for the first time, as if he had had a premonition, which was now coming true in an ecstasy of love at first sight: Galvez's cabin, the wheelhouse by its side, the weeds and puddles, the truck's rusty skeleton, the low wall of rubble, chains, anchors, masts. He recognised that precise tone of grey which only the desperate can pick out in a rainy sky; the thin, purulent line that separated the clouds, the distant, sardonic light strained in the most miserly way. The rain was soaking his hat, but he smiled indulgently without slowing up, trying to make out the furthest sounds of the wind on the river and among the trees. Upright, swaying exaggeratedly, he sidestepped pieces of iron with forgotten shapes and names that lay caught in a mess of wires and entered the darkness, the distant cold, the reticence of the main shed. He examined the racks of shelves, the trickles of rain, the mounds of dust and cobwebs, the red and black machinery that still made a pretence of dignity. He walked noiselessly to the far end of the shed and pushed his buttocks on to the edge of a liferaft. Gazing up at the roof angle — with one eye on the joyful bursts of wind skeetering in, on the archaic rhythms of the rain which had begun to beat on the roof with comic insistence — he felt absent-mindedly for his cigarettes, lit one. He could list everything that did not matter to him: smoking, eating, shelter, other people's respect, the future. He had found something that mid day, or perhaps, after the meeting with Galvez, he had left something forgotten in the General Manager's office. It was all the same.

He smiled to himself as he imagined a noise of rats gnawing at nuts, bolts and spanners in the racks; smiling, he imagined a cosy noon-day in Petrus' house, with a plump, conniving Josefina serving at table, Angelica Ines with her unshakable impersonal smile poking the fire in the fireplace, spoiling an indeterminate number of children while her humble, loving gaze, her plaintive whisper alternated between Larsen's beaming face and her father's great oval portrait, the deceased father-in-law (his head stubborn, arcane and stern, framed by sidewhiskers, looking down from two metres, exemplary, domineering, obeyed.)

Larsen went over to the back door, glanced at the rain's swift, cowardly capitulation, considered the consequences the curtain of fog now rising from the river would have for navigation. He came and went, splashing in the mud and enjoying the sound he made, determinedly contemplating fear, doubt, ignorance, poverty, decline and death. He lit another cigarette and discovered a doorless, abandoned office, with wooden planks for walls. It contained a camp-bed, a box with a book on it, a chipped enamel washbasin. This was Kunz's home.

There's another thing: it never even occurred to me to wonder where the German lived. He went in and sat hunched on the bed, head twisted up towards the door, cigarette clutched against his stomach, in such a humble, friendly attitude that if Kunz were to come in all of a sudden, he could not possibly get angry. *This is real misfortune. It's not bad luck which arrives, insistent, fickle, then moves on, this is misfortune, aged, cold, green as slime. It does not arrive and install itself; it's different, has nothing to do with events, even though it may use them to show itself; sometimes misfortune just is. And it is here now, I don't know since when; I've been going round in circles trying not to notice, I helped it thrive with the dream of being General Manager, the thirty millions, the mouth which laughed without a sound in the summerhouse. Anything I do now will only serve to make it cling tighter still to me. All that's left to do is precisely that: anything, to do one thing after another, without getting involved, as if someone else (or rather other people, one guide for each action) were paying to carry them out, and all one did was to perform as best one could, unconcerned with the final result. One thing, then another, and another, distant, no matter whether they turn out well or badly, no matter what their meaning may be. That is how it has always been; it is better than knocking on wood or being blessed; when misfortune knows the game is up, it starts to dry out, shrivels, and falls off.*

He walked out into the last drops of rain dripping from the blackened plane trees. He went and knocked on the door to Galvez's cabin, and when the woman came to open it (holding the sudden silence at her back, disturbed only by the distant, insignificant sounds of the dogs whining and a foxtrot on the radio) he pushed past her with a lofty "Excuse me" and plunged into the warmth, the men's greeting. He pulled up a stool and sat there, his hat on the dry earth floor, responding to Galvez's boundless smile with his own short, easy, persuasive grin.

"Have you eaten?" the woman asked. "You can't have. Would you like something? There's no lunch left, but I can make you something."

"Thanks. If you had stew," Larsen said, looking at their plates, "perhaps you can spare me a cup of broth or soup."

"I could cook you a steak," the woman said.

"There's plenty of meat," Kunz added.

"No, thanks," Larsen insisted. "Thank you, señora. What I'd really like is a cup of hot broth. I'd be very grateful."

He thought he had overdone his humility; Galvez was staring at him with a mocking look. The woman cleared something from the table, picked up his hat from the floor; he could sense her close behind him, bent thoughtfully over the crackling fire, determined not to speak.

"We're out of wine until tonight," Kunz said. "How about some rum? There's several bottles, it's so foul we never seem to finish it."

"After my soup. Or broth . . ." Larsen replied.

The woman said nothing.

A gust of wind careered loudly twice round the cabin; it flattened the stove's flickering flame. Kunz folded his arms across his chest. "Where did you get to? We thought you had gone to see Petrus."

"Don Jeremias Petrus," Galvez said.

Larsen lifted his head to smile at him, but Galvez was stubbing out his cigarette in a dish. The wind was now whirling furiously right above the cabin. They all fell silent, oppressed by a feeling of distance, heaviness, of swept clouds. The woman put a plate of soup on the table, pushed the dogs away from Larsen's legs.

"Excuse me," Larsen said, and began to spoon up the soup; in front of him, the two watchful men; behind him, the whining dogs and the hostile woman. He stopped eating to gaze at the wooden walls, a clock, a vase with long green handles. "My thanks to you. I wasn't really hungry, but I thought a plate of something hot would do me good. That was why it occurred to me to come and knock here."

"We were just saying you must have gone to Petrus' place," Kunz put in. "And that you wouldn't have found the old man there, for one. I don't think he'll be back till next week."

"We're not worried," Galvez laughed. "They won't allow me to lie. I said we were not worried who you were going to see at Petrus'."

"Galvez," the woman warned from behind Larsen's back.

"If you'll pardon me, it's true we were thinking," Kunz said, "that you might have gone to find the old man this lunchtime to put him on his guard."

"In the rain," Galvez added. "That you were walking to his place to tell him I've got one of the forged certificates, and you got caught by the rain."

"Galvez," the woman said again sternly from somewhere behind Larsen's shoulders.

"That's right," Galvez went on. "That you were going to the house to warn old man Petrus or his daughter. I said — we all said — that it was possible." He produced a jar of rum from between his knees and filled three glasses, pouring the liquor out in a noisy stream. His teeth were not bared, despite the look of permanent amusement on the reddish blob that was his mouth; his tight, unsmiling lips looked naked, as though he had just finished shaving them.

"That you were going in the rain to warn him, and that the warning would be no use at all, because old man Petrus knows it better than any of us, knew it long before we did. We all said so, first one of us, then another. And I added that if that happened, if you made your way to Petrus' house, getting soaked to do your duty — after all, I credit you with six thousand pesos every twenty-fifth of the month — to raise the alarm, then perhaps you were doing me a favour; and that perhaps I have been wanting someone to do me a favour like that for ages."

Larsen gently pushed aside the empty soup plate. He lit a cigarette and leaned forward until he could drink from the glass Galvez had filled.

"Like some more?" the woman asked.

"I've already said no thanks, señora. I came to ask for something hot, an act of charity."

"I was thinking you had probably come up with something new to increase the shipyard profits," Kunz said, almost drowning out Galvez's chuckle. "Something better than fitting out or repairing boats."

"Piracy or prostitution, for example," Galvez suggested. Kunz raised his glass, screwed up his eyes, tilted his head back.

The woman's filthy, chapped hands removed Larsen's plate. The dogs were quiet, asleep perhaps on the enormous bed. The wind stuttered, whistling in the distance; they could all hear it coming and going, forced to make its mind up.

"The problem is whether or not we can count on an agent in El Rosario," Galvez said. "We could double our operations, have a team of pilots to bring the boats up to Puerto Astillero. We could buy ourselves peaked caps, hold serious discussions about bowsprits, prows, foremasts, brig and mizzen sails. We could play at naval battles on the cedarwood table in the Board Room."

He was drinking slumped in the disintegrating wicker chair, his large teeth exposed noncommittally to the smoke-blackened ceiling boards.

"When the rain started," Kunz said, "we were hoping not to have to go to work this afternoon. There's nothing really urgent, is there? Our friend here has the accounts up to date, and the estimates I have to work on can wait. I'm sure you won't mind. We could stay here, drinking, listening to the rain, and talking about Morgan and Drake."

"What d'you say?" Galvez asked.

Larsen finished his rum and stretched out a hand to pour some more; he could sense a stupid grin coming over his face, that his voice would falter if he tried to say anything. The woman brushed past him, past the table and Galvez, then stopped with her face pressed against the moist window-pane; her broad, willing body leaned gently towards the last of the rain.

"I feel better now," Larsen said. He stared neutrally at the back of the woman's head, at her long, unkempt curly hair. "Now. Not because of the soup, which I thank you for, or the rum. Perhaps a bit because you let me in here. I feel better because a while back I glimpsed misfortune, and felt it was mine alone, as though it had only affected me, as if it was inside me and would be there until who knows when. Now I can see it is outside me, affecting others as well; that makes everything easier. Illness is one thing, the plague is something else." He drank half the rum and returned the wary, expectant smile Galvez was offering. The woman still had her back to him and her head down, vaguely hostile.

"Have some more rum," Kunz said. "Listening to the rain and an afternoon siesta. What more could one want?"

"Yes," Larsen said, "that's best for now. But there are always things to be done even if you don't know why you're doing them. It's true, maybe this afternoon I will go to Petrus' place and tell him about the forged certificate. Maybe."

"I've already told you, it wouldn't matter," Galvez responded. The woman drew back from the filthy weather at the smoked-up window; put an arm round Galvez, round the battered armchair, tilted her blank, almost gay face in the direction of the table.

"Tell the old man or the daughter," she muttered.

"Tell the old man or the daugher," Larsen agreed.

THE SHIPYARD IV
THE CABIN IV

Although nobody can now be sure at what point in the story it happened, there is no doubt that there was a week when Galvez refused to go to the shipyard.

For Larsen, Galvez's first morning away must have been the real test of that winter; all the doubts and suffering that came later were far easier to bear.

That morning, Larsen reached the shipyard around ten, greeted Kunz bent in profile over his stamp album at the drawing board, and went into his office already feeling uneasy. He exchanged one pile of files for another and tried to read until eleven, with a sudden light rain dripping from the jagged edges of the broken window-panes. *I've got to worry about myself, nothing more; me, sad and frozen here at my desk, hemmed in by the bad weather, bad luck, the squalor. Yet I do care that this rain is falling on others, beating indifferently on their roofs.*

He got up without a sound and went to the door to peer into the general office. Galvez had not arrived; Kunz was staring out of a window, drinking maté. Larsen mused on the prospect of Galvez's absence being final, so precipitating the end of the delirium which he, Larsen, had taken up like a torch handed to him by earlier, unknown General Managers, and which he had promised to bear until the moment of its unforeseeable outcome. If Galvez had decided to give up the game, it was possible Kunz might be affected. The pair of them, and the woman with her belly and the dogs, might be unable to see the world beyond, the other one, the one everyone else inhabited. But he could.

Larsen waited until it was almost noon, but Kunz never came near the General Manager's door. The drizzle had let up and a dirty, leaden cloud was sitting outside the window, not bothering to advance. Larsen pushed back the files, went over to the window and stuck first one hand and then the other out into the fog. "It can't be," he said over and over to himself. For what was about to happen he would have preferred a previous, earlier time; he would have preferred another kind of faith to see him through. *But we're never allowed to choose, it's only afterwards we realise we could have chosen.* He stroked the trigger on the gun strapped under his arm, ears straining at the harsh silence.

Kunz pushed back his chair and yawned.

Larsen could feel his mouth and cheek twitching as he went back to his desk and put the revolver away in the half-open drawer. "If he tries to be droll, I'll insult him; if he reacts, I'll kill him." He pressed the buzzer to call the Technical Manager in.

"Yes," Kunz shouted, doing up his jacket as he entered.

"Were you leaving? I got caught up in some files I was reading. I lost all track of the time. Do you know anything about the *Tampico* affair?"

"The *Tampico*? Not a thing; it must go back a long way," Kunz replied, with another yawn.

"Yes, the *Tampico*," Larsen insisted. It was only then that he raised his eyes to look at Kunz. He took in his round face with its stubbly cheeks, the shock of stiff black hair, the hairy hand now moving up from the jacket buttons to the black knot of his tie. "It was before your time probably, but it's an interesting precedent. The ship came into the yard in a hurry, fully loaded, with a propeller shaft problem. It seems its cargo was highly inflammable, and it caught fire right here, a bit to the north of the yard. The file says there was no insurance or that not all the cargo was insured." Larsen had opened a file at random and was pretending to read; a rattling drumming on the roof signalled the arrival of more rain. "So, who pays? Who is liable?"

He looked up with a gentle, playful smile, as if he were a child.

"I never heard anything about it," Kunz replied. "And I don't get it. Who knows how long ago it was. It must have made quite a sight, burning on the river. I don't know. But the shipyard can't be held responsible."

"Are you sure?"

"I don't think there's any doubt."

"It's always good to know," Larsen straightened up, ran his fingers with their shiny fingernails along the top of the desk drawer. He sought out Kunz's tiny, dark eyes. "Hasn't Galvez been in this morning?"

"No, I haven't seen him. We went to El Chamamé last night. But he was in good shape when I left him."

"Has he sent in a sick note?"

"You mean did he tell anyone? It's raining. I'm going to drop by his house now." Kunz suddenly looked at Larsen with interest. "If he didn't come, he must be ill. The problem is we were expecting the Jews with their truck this afternoon. He promised to give me a hand with the bargaining." He raised a hand in farewell, then from the doorway turned to give Larsen's face a lingering, gloating scrutiny.

"Something wrong?" he whispered.

"Nothing," Larsen replied. As soon as the other man had left, he let his breath out in a long sigh.

He did not have lunch at the cabin. Instead he ate a piece of meat in silence at the Belgrano, refusing to respond to any of the topics the owner suggested from behind the bar. At five o'clock he made his way through the puddles to go and see Galvez; by now he was a model of tolerance; magnanimous, paternal.

The woman was sitting on the front steps, wrapped in her overcoat, with one dog on her lap and the other with its snout pushed up against her heavy shoe. Her sodden face glistened tranquilly in the murky fog. Larsen cursed himself for coming, began to feel that he was dark and clumsy, an intruder. As he touched his hat brim in greeting he found himself forced to change his mind about the woman's age. The two of them, exhausted, disbelieving, were at the centre of a cloud. No sounds filtered through to their rescue.

"You're young enough to be my daughter," Larsen conceded, taking off his hat.

The silence deepened still further, as though freed from the murmuring that nibbled at its edges. The dog on the ground stretched and wagged its tail. The woman was scratching the chest of the dog on her lap. Beneath the thick red line of the scarf round her neck, the lapels of her coat were fastened with a huge safety pin. Her face's gentleness was unfocused; the corner of her pale, fleshy mouth turned slackly upwards at the tips; her half-closed eyes made no pretence at seeing anything. Larsen noted her outsize men's shoes, tied with electric cable and caked with mud and leaves.

"Señora," he said. Her smile widened, but her eyes were still unseeing, and the mist was coagulating in little drops on them; "Señora, very soon, everything will sort itself out."

"You don't say," she laughed, her mouth open wide. "Go in and give him a lecture, or tell him a nice story. He decided to take it out on himself, going to bed and turning his face to the wall. He's not even pretending to be asleep. He's not ill either. I told him how dreadful it would be if you sent the company doctor along and he found out there was nothing wrong with him. They might decide to sack him, I said, and we'd be forced to go and live in some wooden shack, a ship's wheelhouse or a dog kennel. Go on in and try your luck; perhaps he has died, perhaps he will deign to talk to you. Anyway, there's a bottle."

Hampered by the cold and damp, Larsen was unable to find the right words to explain to the woman how much he cared for her, how in some strange, harassed way the two of them had been brother and sister even during the long years of separation from and ignorance of each other. He put his hat back on, and walked towards the woman as if he were obeying an order, stooping slightly to ask for forgiveness.

She moved aside. Larsen carefully climbed the three circus caravan steps attached for no good reason to the cabin side by an iron chain. He stepped into the grey gloom and had no trouble finding his way over to the corner where the bed stood.

Galvez was facing the wooden planks of the wall; there was the sound of breathing, doubtless his eyes were open.

"How are things?" Larsen eventually said in an insincere voice.

"Why don't you go to hell?" Galvez suggested sweetly.

Larsen controlled the intensity of the indignation he felt justified in experiencing. He dragged a bench over with his foot and was bending over to sit down when he caught sight of the bottle on the table. It was almost full, with a picture of grapes, an ear of corn and feathers on the label. He poured himself some in a tin mug, and sat staring at the narrow back concealed under the patched, clean sheet.

"You can tell me to go as often as you like. I won't leave because I need to talk to you. This brandy is foul, would you like some?"

He took another sip and looked around him; he was thinking that the cabin was part of the whole game, that it had been built and lived in solely to put on scenes that could not be staged in the shipyard.

"We're nearly there; I've been given permission to tell you. A few more days and the shipyard will start up again. We'll have not only the legal authority but all the money we need as well. Millions of pesos. We may need to change the company by adding another name to Petrus', or by using some other name that isn't a surname. I won't bother to mention the wages we're owed; the new Board acknowledges them and will honour them. Neither Petrus nor I would have had it any other way. So you can start calculating. That should take care of things and allow us to live decently, as we deserve. But our future wages are what's really important. Oh, and one more thing: the housing units the company is going to build for its employees. Of course, no one will be obliged to live in them, but they'll be very convenient. I'll soon be able to show you the plans. I have Petrus' word on all this."

Needless to say, he did not have it; all he had was his tedious mania, the spell he was under and had to carry out, his need to make all this last. In the cold, grimy cabin, drinking without getting drunk in response to the Administrative Manager's indifference, Larsen felt the terror of lucidity. Beyond the farce he had accepted as if it were a job, there was nothing but the winter, old age, nowhere to go, the possibility of death. He would have given anything to see Galvez sit up in bed, flash a toothy grin, and start to drink from the bottle.

Refusing to admit defeat, he spoke of himself, repeated the monologues he pronounced in Petrus' summerhouse. He was in the middle of a lying acount of his meeting with Inspector Vales, the gun on the desk, the offensive way he spat, when Galvez stretched out his legs, turned to face him, yawning.

"Why don't you go to hell?" he suggested again. "I'll be back at work tomorrow."

They laughed together, without merriment; they preferred a serious note. Then they lapsed into silence, sitting still for a long while, thinking about the truth. The dogs had been barking furiously but soon could no longer be heard. Larsen had not wasted his afternoon; he was staying on now to be polite, dissembling. He picked up the bottle and went to leave it on the table; he did not say goodbye because he put no trust in words.

It was surprisingly dark as he made his way cautiously down the three steps and swayed his rolling walk across the empty lot. No sign of the woman or dogs. A light-hearted wind was sweeping the sky clear; by midnight it seemed certain the stars would be out.

SANTA MARIA II

The last southbound ferry called at Puerto Astillero at four twenty and reached Santa Maria around five.

Slow as the early morning one, it had an awning raised to keep off the rain and drew up at every landing stage to leave off eggs, demijohns of wine, letters and greetings, a confused message tossed over the choppy waves before any attempt to reach the riverbank. But at five o'clock, whatever the weather was like, it would still be light in Santa Maria, and there would be onlookers at the jetty. Larsen had no wish — above all since he knew he was going there for nothing, that his journey was only a meaningless break, an empty action — to have to walk up the cobbles of the harbour, the steep inclines of the narrow lanes, his eyes seeking out any looks of astonishment, taunts or simple recognition, his mouth clamped shut but loaded with a string of prepared insults, his hand hypocritically half-hidden in his lapel, his finger on the trigger, stroking it endlessly with feigned fury, ready for anything.

Anyway, perhaps I won't be able to find Diaz Grey, perhaps he's croaked or is away in La Colonia waiting by lantern light to see if a cow or a dumb immigrant woman finally decides to heave out her placenta. He's stupid enough. If I'm looking for him on today of all days, in this weather, when there is nothing to prevent me postponing my journey apart from the superstition that movement, blind and perpetual, might grind down misfortune, it is because more than anyone else he possesses that quality which in haste I call stupidity.

So he walked down the muddy road from Puerto Astillero to Belgrano's upright in the wind, hanging on to his hat with two fingers. He went up to his room, surveyed himself in the mirror, decided to have a shave and change his tie. "That quality which shines out constantly from his small, placid face, heaven knows what to call it. That makes you feel sorry for him, like slapping him on the back, calling him brother, Diaz Grey."

He went downstairs to share a drink with the owner. From the bar he glanced at the knots of customers in the dank, smoke-filled room. He saw an old man with two younger men, wearing leather jackets and oilskin capes. They were drinking white wine next to a window; one of the youths kept parting his lips to show his teeth; he wiped the window with his forearm, smiling as he did so at his friends, at the grey, swirling afternoon outside.

"What can they be fishing in this weather?" Larsen asked, feigning interest.

"You'd be surprised," the proprietor said. "It all depends on the currents. Sometimes when the water is muddy they catch more than they can handle."

When the clock high on the wall with the faded aperitif advert on its dial showed half past four, Larsen tapped himself on the forehead, put his hands on the counter.

"Gott," the owner said, straightening up, dishcloth in hand. "What did you forget?"

Larsen shook his head then smiled, putting on a brave front.

"Nothing to speak of. I had a really important meeting in Santa Maria tonight. And the last boat left some time ago. Yes, something really important."

"Ah," the proprietor said. "I get it. Josefina was here at lunchtime. She told me in confidence that don Jeremias was arriving in Santa Maria tonight. At midnight."

"That's right," Larsen concurred. "But now there's nothing I can do. Shall we have another?"

"Yes, the last boat's at twenty past four. It might not seem much, but there used to be only one a week, then two. When it went up to two, we threw a party right here." He filled the glasses carefully, with restrained emotion. "Who knows. Excuse me . . ." he raised his glass, took a sip, and went to sit with the fishermen.

Alone at the bar, head cocked at the storm and the river, at the hidden source of the stench of decay, of depths thrown to the surface, of dead memories, which were seeping into the Belgrano, Larsen thought about life, about women, about the wind rustling in the bare branches of the plane trees, around the gigantic dog kennel behind the shipyard. "Now look, just as everything is coming to an end: the crazy woman and her laughter in the summerhouse, and that creature in her man's overcoat done up with a safety pin. They are one woman really, exactly the same. There never were different women, only one woman repeated over and over in exactly the same way. There were hardly any variations possible, there was no way I could be caught unawares. So everything, from the first dance in the local club right to the end, was made easy for me, downhill all the way, all I had to spend were time and patience."

Smiling, his thumb crooked round his empty glass, the owner returned to the bar.

"Another one?"

"No thanks," Larsen said. "I've had my fill."

"Suit yourself." He aimlessly wiped the dry wood with the grimy cloth. "I've found something. If it's as important as I think it is for you to see Petrus tonight . . . it won't be very comfortable, but it's all there is. Our friends over there are from Miguez, the other side of Enduro, where the sea begins."

"I know the place," Larsen said casually, standing in silhouette, the cigarette dangling from the corner of his mouth.

"If you're up to it . . . I've talked to them and they'd be happy to take you as far as Santa Maria. It'll be rough, and there's no awning. Think about it; they won't charge you."

Larsen smiled without turning to the three men, without acknowledging their glances and timid nods of encouragement.

"Is it a sailboat?"

"They've got a motor," the proprietor replied. "It's the Laura — you must have seen it. But of course if there's no need, they won't waste diesel."

"Thanks," Larsen muttered. "When are they leaving?"

"Right away. They were about to set off."

"Fine. Lend me fifty till Monday if you can and will. We'll settle up on Monday."

The proprietor opened his till and rapped the green banknote on the counter. Larsen nodded, twisting it between two fingers. Treading lightly to appear less bulky, hands in pockets and the cigarette, by now almost entirely ash, still dangling from his friendly, fraternal mouth, Larsen sauntered over to the fishermen. They all stood up, smiling and nodding. So began Larsen's journey to Santa Maria.

Hagen, the attendant at the petrol station on the corner of the square, thought he recognised him. It must have been that same night; it was raining and none of the statements suggests that after moving to Puerto Astillero Larsen made any other visit to Santa Maria apart from his very last trip and this one, more confused and open to speculation.

"I thought it was Larsen by the way he walked. There was hardly any light, and the rain was a nuisance. I wouldn't have seen him, or imagined I had, but for the fact that the truck from the shoe factory, which usually passes by in the afternoon, chose that precise moment — almost ten o'clock at night — to turn up. He honked his horn until I was forced to come out of the Nueva Italia; the driver and I were swapping insults until I said to him: 'Hang on a minute', with the pump in my hand, and I stared at the corner I thought I had seen Larsen emerge from. Like I told you, it had been raining again, and the street lamp at the corner gave out next to no light. He was soaked, and looked older, if it was him; he used his arms to help himself along more than he used to, head down, his black homburg pulled over his face against the rain, and so I couldn't make out his features. Always supposing it was him. They said he was in the capital, and I can vouch for the fact that he didn't arrive on the noon ferryboat or the afternoon one; if he came on the seven minutes past five train I'd have known. So it was for less than half a block, with the light and the rain making things difficult, from the corner they're demolishing to build a tyre showroom they reckon, as if there weren't enough of them already, until his figure was hidden behind the doctor's car and he must have turned into a doorway. I'm sure of that, because what light there was glinted off the brass plate, which he's never once had polished since he became a doctor. If Larsen turned at that corner, he hadn't come from the ferry or from the railway station. Only half a block, or less; and there were all the difficulties I've mentioned. But though I wouldn't swear to it, I reckon it was him; above all, I recognised that swaggering walk of his, though it has less of a spring in it these days, and something I can't quite explain about the way he moves his arms, with his shirt cuffs sticking out of his short coat sleeves. Thinking it over later, that was what made me think my hunch was right: in that cold and rain, anyone else would have kept their hands in their pockets. But not him; if it was him."

The time at which Hagen had his dubious sighting of Larsen coincided with the moment when Dr Diaz Grey (following a desultory after dinner read as he sat alone while the maid cleared away the dishes, smoothed out the green baize cloth and put a pack of cards next to him) usually began to wonder what method he could try in order to get to sleep, what combination of drugs, rhythmic breathing, tricks of the imagination. Perhaps it was not him doing the wondering but a faithful memory, somewhere inside him, independent of him for many years now. And always, with a curt gesture of pointless defiance that made him feel young again, he decided not to do anything, to wait as still as possible for the dawn, then morning, then another night to follow on from this one.

If no patient called him out, obliging him to go clattering off at comic speed in the second or third hand jalopy he had eventually felt obliged to buy, this was the time when he put sacred music on the record player and settled to play games of patience, only bestowing on the music, which he knew by heart and was always identical, always played in the same order, no more than a quarter of his attention, while he hesitated, mildly excited, between kings and aces, seconal and bromide.

Each of the records in his unchanging night-time recital, each of its soaring crescendos and collapsing finales, had a precise meaning, expressed with greater precision than could be encompassed in word or thought. But he, Diaz Grey, this Santa Maria doctor, a confirmed bachelor of nearly fifty, going bald, poor, accustomed by now to boredom and the shamefaced feeling of happiness, could not lend the music — that very music, chosen partly as a challenge, from the perverse desire to sense each night, sheltered from danger, that he was on the verge of the truth and inevitable annihilation — more than a quarter of his attention. Sometimes, deliberately mischievous, he whistled the music through clenched teeth, while he proudly and firmly changed a seven or a jack from one row to another.

At ten that night, the one Hagen talked of or any other, Diaz Grey heard the street doorbell ring. He jumbled up the cards as though trying to cover his tracks, and stopped the record that was playing. *If they don't telephone at this time of night it's because it's an urgent case. They're desperate to catch the doctor at all costs, the superstitious relief that comes from seeing and talking to him as soon as possible. Perhaps it's Freitas — he's in his last week; if it is, prescribe digitalis and talk with his stupid children about their flax crops, with the youngest about his thoroughbred racehorse. If he dies in the early hours I'll offer them my tiredness, my insomnia and my patience until dawn.* He went from the dining-room to the surgery, and when he reached the hall shouted to the woman he could hear coming down the stairs from her room above:

"Don't worry, I'll get it."

Two metres below, at the storm door that was never locked, Larsen doffed his hat to shake off the rain, smiled an apologetic smile of greeting.

"Come on up," Diaz Grey said. He went into the consulting room, leaving the door open. He leaned on his desk waiting for Larsen, listening to the squelching sound as his shoes climbed the stairs, trying to rekindle the memories associated with his gruff voice, his lopsided smile.

"Greetings," Larsen said in the doorway, taking off his hat a second time. "I'm going to ruin your floor." He stepped forward and smiled again, but this time with no hint of humility or even courtesy, his head tilted to one side, his round, calculating eyes sunk in deep furrows. "Remember me?"

Diaz Grey remembered everything. He was still standing at the desk, chewing his lips as he felt a warmth for his memories mingled with an absurd sense of pity for this man who stood silently dripping rainwater on to the linoleum. He shook hands with him, clapped him on his soaking, frozen shoulder.

"Why don't you take your coat off and sit down? I've got an electric fire. Shall I bring it in?" He felt protective, stronger than

Larsen, with nothing to prove, and with no qualms about showing it.

Larsen said not to bother. He struggled out of his coat, then went and left it with his hat on the doctor's couch.

But he's never been here. He never brought me any of his women for a useless examination of their insides. Perhaps he came one evening, before antibiotics existed, to ask me with false pride, between friends, to use the scrape on him. Yet he's moving about the room as if he knew everything in it, as if this visit was a repeat of many earlier nights.

"Doctor," Larsen said gruffly, falsely solemn, looking him in the eye.

Diaz Grey pushed a chrome chair towards him, went to sit behind his desk. *The screen in the corner behind his left shoulder; the couch where he laid out his coat like a dead man, the hat covering a smooth, invisible face; the bookshelves; the windows the rain is beating at again.*

"Long time no see," he said.

"Years," Larsen agreed. "Cigarette? Of course, you hardly ever smoked, did you?" He lit his own cigarette, with a spurt of annoyance because he felt that something was getting away from him, that he was isolated and exposed in the uncomfortable metal and leather chair in the middle of the consulting room. "Look here, first I'd like to apologise for all the mess I got you into back then. You behaved impeccably, though you had no reason to, though the whole business meant nothing to you. Thanks again."

"No," Diaz Grey said slowly, determined to get all he could out of the night and their meeting. "I simply did what seemed right to me at the time, what I had to do. Did you know that Father Bergner died?"

"I read it some time ago. He had been promoted, hadn't he? I heard they'd given him another post in the provincial capital."

"No, he never left here. He didn't want to go. When he became ill, he was my patient."

"You won't believe me but, after it was all over, I came to the conclusion that the priest was a good man. He was doing his job and I mine."

"Wait a minute," the doctor said, standing up. "I've got something that'll do you good after getting soaked like that."

He went to the dining-room and returned with a bottle of rum and two glasses. As he poured their drinks, he listened to the fine screen of rain on the window, to the silence of the countryside beyond; he shuddered, felt a desire to smile like a child being read stories.

"Contraband," Larsen mused, raising the bottle.

"I suppose so, they bring it in on the ferry," Diaz Grey sat behind the desk again, reassured and able to protect himself with indifference, as though Larsen were a patient. "Wait," he said again, as the other man lifted the glass to his lips. He walked over to his instrument cabinet, disconnected the telephone, then went back to his seat at the desk.

"It's good. Dry," Larsen said.

"Help yourself. So that's what you decided about the Father. I thought then, and still do, that you and he were very similar. Of course the similarity would take a long while to explain. Anyway, all that is ancient history. There must have been a reason for your coming here tonight. I didn't know you were in Santa Maria."

"No, doctor," Larsen said, refilling the glasses, "fortunately I'm in excellent health. And I'm not in Santa Maria. Believe me, I would never have come back here if I hadn't wanted to see you. Let me explain," he raised his eyes and once more sketched the lopsided grin that was his smile. "I am in Puerto Astillero, at Petrus' place. He offered me the manager's job, and I took it."

"I see," Diaz Grey nodded cautiously, fearful that Larsen might fall silent again, incredulous but thankful at what the night had brought him. He drank, smiling as though he understood and approved of everything. "Yes, I know old man Petrus and his daughter. I have clients and friends in Puerto Astillero."

He took another drink to conceal his satisfaction, and asked Larsen for a cigarette even though he had a box full of them on the desk. Yet he had no desire to make fun of anyone, and no one in particular seemed to him laughable. It was just that he felt an unusual, warm thrill of simple gratitude that the life men led was just as absurd and senseless as ever, and in one way or another went on sending him envoys gratuitously to confirm its absurdity, its senselessness.

"A very responsible position," he said neutrally. "Especially just now, when the firm is in difficulties. Had Petrus known you long?"

"No, he knows nothing about my past. Nobody in Puerto Astillero does. It was more of a chance meeting, doctor. I took the liberty of giving your name as a reference."

"They never got in touch with me." Diaz Grey took another sip and listened to the rain. He was filled with a comfortable, unanxious kind of curiosity. He stopped looking at Larsen, stopped talking, and let his gaze roam over the spines of the books on the shelves. Larsen cleared his throat in the silence.

"Just two things. A couple of questions to put to you, doctor. I know you're someone I can talk to."

This man old before his time, the Bodysnatcher, with his high blood pressure, a gentle gleam on his balding skull, sitting there with his legs wide apart and his paunch spreading over his lap.

"If it's about Petrus," Diaz Grey said, "He's sleeping in the Plaza Hotel, at the corner of the square. I spoke to him just this afternoon."

"I already knew that, doctor," Larsen said with a smile. "Believe it or not, that's not why I'm here."

This man who has lived for the past thirty years on filthy money gladly offered him by filthy women, who has had the strength to defend himself against life by replacing it with an unheralded betrayal combining toughness and audacity; who held one belief and now holds another, who was not born to die but to win and to impose himself, who at this very moment is imagining life as an infinite, timeless region across which he must advance and conquer something.

"Ask whatever you like. Wait a minute." He went into the dining-room and switched the record player back on; he left the door half-closed, so the sound of the music was no louder than the rain.

"First of all the firm, doctor. What do you reckon? You must know. I mean, is it likely that Petrus Ltd. will manage to recover?"

"That's what they've been asking themselves in Santa Maria for the past five years over their drinks at the hotel and in the club. I have some information, but you're on the spot; you're the Manager."

Larsen's mouth twisted again into a smile. He looked down at his fingernails. The two men gazed at each other; the sound of the rain had stopped; in its place choir music filled the consulting-room. A ship's languid hoot echoed across the river.

"Like in church," Larsen nodded, gently and respectfully. "I'll be frank with you. I have nothing to do with the administrative side of things. At the moment I'm carrying out a general survey so that I can get to know the company properly; I'm also looking at costs." He shrugged apologetically. "The place is in ruins."

This man of all men, who was meant to stay at least a hundred kilometres from here until the day of his death, found he had to come back and get his stiff legs caught in what is left of Petrus' spider-web.

"As far as I know," Diaz Grey said, "there isn't the slightest hope. They haven't wound up the company yet because nobody would gain anything by it. The major shareholders gave it up as a bad job a long time ago and have forgotten about it."

"Are you sure? Petrus talks about thirty million."

"Yes, I know, that's what he said to me this afternoon. Petrus is crazy, or is trying to go on believing in order to avoid going crazy.

If they do wind up the company, he'll get a hundred thousand pesos and I know that he, personally, owes over a million. But until then he can go on presenting documents and visiting ministries. He's very old by now anyway. Do you receive a salary?"

"Not in any real sense, for the moment."

"I see," Diaz Grey said gently. "I met some of Petrus' other managers; several of them came to say goodbye in Santa Maria while they were waiting for the ferry. A long list, and no two the same. As if Petrus chose them or had them chosen for their dissimilarities, in the hope one day of finding someone different from all other men, someone who might even thrive on disillusion and hunger, who might never leave."

"You may be right, doctor."

"I saw them with my own eyes."

(In three years, there may have been five or six of these managers, general, administrative, or technical, from Jeremias Petrus Ltd. who had passed through Santa Maria on their return from an exile which they could not think of as a mere distancing from places familiar, or at least capable of being known and understood, to them. Not so different after all; akin to each other in their poverty, the aggressive wretchedness of their outlandish, ill-matched clothing. But all with an air of closely observed decay, something they all wore as a uniform in the tiny army created by Petrus' contagious madness. Perhaps twice as many had not been seen in Santa Maria, making fresh contact with a world that was cruel and hostile but which could be believed, and challenged. Some of them caught a ferry in Puerto Astillero and headed off in other directions; others passed through the city still prey to a fear that might have been mistaken for pride and made them seem anonymous and invisible. Not so different; alike too in their gaze, not so much empty as emptied of all they had known and believed in, of everything that still filled the eyes of the inhabitants of this first piece of ground they set foot on in their flight.

As all those who spoke with them knew, and as they themselves admitted, they were in fact returning from Puerto Astillero, a place like any other on the river, with its German settlers and its half-breed shacks clustered around the building which housed Petrus Ltd., a grey cube of flaking cement, a ruin dotted with rusty iron shapes. They were on their way back from a spot that was only a few minutes away from Santa Maria by boat, or a little over two hours on foot for a determined or desperate man who could force his way through the barbed wire of farms, the reed beds. They all shared the same eyes, when they turned away from the kindly people who listened to their vague, passionate ramblings; their eyes linked them to all the other kinds of manager who had beaten a retreat through the city, to all those who would do so in the future. Their gaze, with a surprisingly hard but joyful gleam in it. They, the managers, were back; they were thankful to be able to touch wood, hands, windows, thankful for the mouths which asked them questions, the smiles, the expressions of pity and amazement.

Yet this gleam of triumph in their eyes was not due to the return from exile, or not only that. Their gaze spoke of coming back to life, of being sure that the memory of the death they had so recently left behind — an incommunicable memory, hostile to both words and silence — would forever more be part and parcel of their souls. Their eyes said they were not returning from any precise place; rather, they were back from having been nowhere, in an absolute solitude misleadingly peopled with symbols: ambition, security, time, power. Never entirely lucid, never wholly free, they were back from a private hell unwittingly created by old man Petrus.)

The music spoke of fraternity and consolation. Head on one side, his glass clasped between his knees, Larsen listened good-naturedly, but without belief in any meaning or conceivable outcome from this meeting, certain only that to endure was to triumph.

"Rest assured, doctor. None of us is going to die of hunger. I've organised the people there, the senior staff who are left, and we've no reason to complain. I'm not thinking of quitting."

"Yes, perhaps you are the man Petrus needed, the right man for him. There's nothing funny or unbelievable about that, although it's true I would have laughed if anyone else had told me so. Strange that nobody here knew anything."

"Puerto Astillero is dead, doctor. The ferries hardly bother to call there, nobody comes or goes. I had to hire a fishing boat to get here today." Larsen smiled scornfully and apologetically; the next record was a convincing paean to absurd hope.

"So you're up there," Diaz Grey said, suddenly exultant. "Everything is fine, as it should be. Let me talk; I hardly ever drink, apart from the evening aperitif at the hotel bar. And always, almost always, the same people, the same things. You and Petrus. I should have foreseen it; I see that now and I'm ashamed of myself. Life holds no surprises, you know. The things which surprise us are the very things which confirm the meaning of life. But we have been badly prepared, we demand to be badly prepared for that. Perhaps not you or Petrus." Diaz Grey smiled and filled Larsen's glass on the desk, and then his own, slowly, the smile of veiled compassion still etched on his face. He heard the record player click in the silence: only one side of the record was left; the rain and wind had ceased.

"Make that the last, doctor," Larsen said. "I've still got things — very important things — to do tonight. You can't imagine how pleased I am to see you and be here with you. I've always thought and said that Dr Diaz Grey was the best there is. Your health. You're right, life holds no surprises; at least not for real men. We know life inside out, like we know women, if you'll allow me the comparison. As for the meaning of life, don't imagine I'm talking nonsense. I know a thing or two. We do things, but can't possibly do more than we do. Or to put it another way, we don't always choose. As for the others . . ."

"The others too, believe me," the doctor said in the composed, clear and straightforward tone he had been taught at university to adopt when speaking to poor patients. "You and them. Every single one of us is well aware our way of life is farcical, able to admit as much but refusing to do so because we also need to protect our own personal farce. I'm no exception, of course. Petrus is a joker when he offers you the post of General Manager, you are one when you accept. It's a game, and both you and he know the other is playing it. But you keep quiet and pretend. Petrus needs a manager as a bargaining chip so that he can say the shipyard never ceased functioning. You want your wages to go on accumulating just in case some day the miracle happens, things work out, and you can demand payment. That's my interpretation, anyway."

It was the last track of the record. It pleaded for belief in an alienated kind of acceptance that could never spontaneously occur in a man. *It doesn't matter if he doesn't understand. I have a hunch I'll never see him again. I can talk, not to him, not to what he knows, but to what he used to mean to me.*

"You win, doctor. About that. But there's something else." Larsen smiled as though he were publicly thanking the doctor, keeping the best part of that something else well hidden: his own madness, his projects for metallisation, his estimates for repairing the hulls of ships now perhaps buried in a watery grave, his lonely dreams in the ruined shed; his enslaved, ardent love for all the objects, the unlived memories, the souls in torment which inhabited the shipyard.

"Of course. If there weren't, you'd already be in the hotel with Petrus. You say, Larsen, that we are not always what we do. You may be right. I'm thinking about what we said before, about the meaning of life. The mistake is that we think the same about life, that it is not what it does. That's a lie; that is exactly what it is, what all of us see and know" — but he couldn't bring himself to say it, and so merely thought: "and there's a clear meaning to this, a meaning which life itself has never tried to hide, a meaning against which men have stupidly fought since time immemorial with their words and anxieties. And the proof of mankind's inability to accept the true meaning of life lies in the fact that the most incredible of all possibilities, our own death, is mere routine for life; an event which at every moment has already happened."

The needle scratched in the silence at the end of the record. There was another click, then a peaceful calm. Diaz Grey felt empty, bored. He wondered at his vague sense of regret.

"You must be right, doctor. But I for one never went looking for complications. Yes, there is something else." Larsen stared down at his shoes dulled by the wet, pulled at his socks. "Do you know Petrus' daughter? Angelica Ines. We're engaged to be married."

Unable to laugh, toying with the idea that this meeting was a dream or at the very least a comedy staged for him by someone unknown just to make him happy for a few hours one night, Diaz Grey sank back in his chair, plucking a cigarette from the box on the desk.

"Angelica Ines Petrus," he murmured. "And only a short while ago I said hesitatingly, without conviction — you and Petrus. I think it's perfect; everything is perfect on reflection."

"Thank you, doctor. There's a problem. You probably know . . ." Not really hoping or intending to be believed, as a simple act of friendly homage, Larsen stopped staring at his feet and lifted his eyes to meet the doctor's gaze, putting on the most convincing air of innocence, of honest concern and sincerity that he could muster at the age of fifty. Diaz Grey nodded, as if the loathsome, impersonal attempt to win sympathy that showed on Larsen's features had been spoken out loud. He waited expectantly. "We love each other of course. It all began from next to nothing, as these things always do. But this is a serious step. The main reason for me coming here, with this weather and in a fishing boat, was to talk to you about the problem. There may be children, marriage might be harmful for her."

"When is the wedding?" Diaz Grey asked eagerly.

"Exactly. You must realise I can't keep her waiting. I'd like to know, as far as professional secrecy allows you to . . ."

"Well," Diaz Grey said, leaning forward, first yawning and then smiling calmly, tears clouding his eyes. "She is odd. Not normal. She is mad, but it is quite possible she'll never get any worse than she is now. Children are out of the question. Her mother died raving mad, although the actual cause was a stroke. And as I said, old man Petrus is feigning madness in order not to go completely mad. I'm sorry to have to say it, but it would be better not to have children. As for living with her, I imagine you know what she is like, so you will know if you can stand it."

He stood up, yawned once more. Larsen rapidly crumpled his look of worried innocence and, knees creaking, went over to the couch to pick up his coat and hat.

Now, in the incomplete reconstruction of that night, in the quirky desire to give this some historic importance or meaning, in the harmless pastime of shortening a winter's night by confusing and ensnaring with all these things of no interest to anyone and entirely dispensable, it is time for the account given by the Plaza Hotel barman.

He accepts that one rainy night that winter a man corresponding to the description he was given of Larsen, a detailed though in some instances contradictory description (different people stressing different things) came up to the bar and asked if señor Jeremias Petrus was "putting up at" the hotel.

"It was an old fashioned expression, so I stopped thinking about Simmons' Fizz and looked at him again. Nowadays, nearly everyone talks of 'staying' or 'being' in a hotel, though some of the older generation from La Colonia still say 'stopping over'. But this fellow said 'put up at'. He kept his hands in his coat pockets, and did not take off his hat. He didn't say 'good evening' either, or maybe I didn't hear him. That old fashioned expression, perhaps with a bit of help from his voice, made me think of my youth, of street corner cafés. Those things. When he spoke I had nothing to do, the room was almost empty, nobody at the bar, I was wiping the odd glass with the cloth though that's not my job and the glasses are always clean anyway. I was thinking about the black barman Charlie Simmons, of the fizz he had invented, of the proof that the recipe he gave me for it was false, because he told me it straightaway, because the drink it makes looks beautiful but tastes awful, because I never really saw him prepare it. At the time, though not for long, he was working in the Ricky, the place that became the Noneim, and then something else. My mind was half on that and on other things gone by. Then the man came in, maybe the one you're referring to, though I never saw him before, when he was living in Santa Maria. He wasn't that tall, but sure of himself, putting on weight, old age on the horizon but still solid, with an air of paying no heed to the passing days. I should have told him to go and ask the porter Tobias, the one who keeps the guest list and the keys. But that expression, if Petrus was 'putting up at' the hotel, the words he used, won me over and I answered him. I said he was, and told him which room. We all knew and talked about it: old man Petrus ill or pretending to be, shut since morning in number 25, the suite with a sitting-room that's normally kept for newlyweds, without ordering anything but a bottle of mineral water. None of us knew, whatever they said, whether the Frenchman would dare present Petrus with his bill, several thousand pesos altogether, for this stay and all the previous ones. And not just so that he could sign for the account, but actually get him to add his signature to a valid cheque, drawn on a bank that I can't quite conceive of but which, why not, could be called Petrus and Co., or Petrus and Petrus. The man nodded in thanks and walked off towards the lift. I wanted to call him to tell him to use the internal phone, but I did nothing and he went on his way. He was just like you describe him: naturally heavy, but somehow accentuating it; dressed in black; his footsteps echoing in the silence of the empty bar until they were muffled by the corridor carpet, his back arched as if he were pushing something along with his chest. Poor man. The other thing I was thinking about was something that might have occurred to anyone. I was thinking about Charlie Simmons the black barman, the smartest dresser I've ever seen, about the time, which must have happened, when he was absentmindedly stirring a gin fizz with a long spoon and suddenly realised that it could be done better, or that it was possible to become famous just by changing the proportions or ingredients without adding anything new or better. Just how he did it I don't know. I still wonder about it."

The door was not locked, so after a few tentative steps through the darkened sitting-room, Larsen stepped into the light of the bedroom and saw Petrus propped up on his back, filling barely a quarter of the bed. He had a pen in his hand; a black notebook with chrome rings rested on his knees. His wizened face was turned towards Larsen. It betrayed no astonishment or fear, nothing apart from a mild professional curiosity.

"Good evening and excuse me," Larsen said. He took his hands from his pockets and carefully placed his hat on the shelf of the fake mantelpiece.

"So it's you, is it?" the old man commented. He pushed his pen and notebook under the pillow without turning his head.

"Yes, here I am, in spite of everything. And I'm afraid that ..." he stepped forward quickly, holding out his hand for Petrus to place his own small, dry palm in his.

"Yes," Petrus said. "Do sit down. Bring up a chair." He looked Larsen over, nodding his head as if approving of what he saw.

"I trust everything is going well at the shipyard. Our triumph is at hand, it's only a matter of days. So sad that in times like these a simple act of justice should be called a triumph. A government minister has given me his word. Any problems with the staff?"

Larsen sat on the bed. He smiled to ingratiate himself with the angels, thought of the legion of ghosts who made up the staff, of traces they might have left but which in no way could be taken as proof; he thought of Galvez and Kunz, of the two dogs jumping up at the belly of the woman in her man's overcoat. Also of puddles, a gaping hole in the shape of a window, a door hinge hanging loose.

"None at all. There was a certain absurd reluctance to begin with. But now I can assure you, everything is going like clockwork."

Petrus smiled and said that was exactly what he had expected and that he knew he never made a mistake when he chose people and gave them a job to do. "I am a leader; that is a leader's chief asset." The night lay outside, reduced to silence; the world's immensity could be called into question.

Inside there was nothing more than the skinny body under the blankets, the yellow skull smiling out from the thick vertical pillows, the old man and his game.

"I'm glad," Larsen said evenly, credulous. "I have always felt that while I was taking care of the problems at the shipyard and making sure the staff pulled their weight, I was commanding the rearguard whereas you were . . ." he sighed, almost contented, and shivered in his sodden overcoat.

". . . in the line of fire. Quite right," the old man smiled in self-congratulation. "Greater risks, greater glory. But if the rearguard should fail . . ."

"That's what gives me strength."

"My work is here," Petrus said, slipping his hand under the pillow to touch the notebook. "And I'm not going to die before I see that everything has started up again. Impossible. But your task is just as important as mine. If the shipyard should cease to function for even one hour, what would I be defending in the waiting rooms of those bureaucrats, those upstarts? I'm very grateful to you."

Larsen smiled a timid, thankful grin of gratitude. Petrus quickly took in the smile and his thin face between its sidewhiskers began to take on a deliberately expectant expression, polite but firm.

A man and a woman went past the door talking out loud; the man was denying something, scornfully, drawing on reserves of patience.

"I can assure you, everything is ready, waiting for the moment when you give the order," Larsen put in.

But neither the voices outside the room nor the one which had come to him from the foot of the bed could distract the head lolling weightlessly like a mummified monkey on the pillows from its determined interrogation.

That split furrow he is making is no smile. He couldn't care less about anyone. I am not who I am, nor even the thirtieth or fortieth body who tonight is the unchanging General Manager of the shipyard. I am no more than an object of distrust. He isn't even afraid of me. It's late, I came in without knocking, he did not tell me he would be in Santa Maria. He'd like to know why I am lying, what plans and hopes I have. He's impatient to find out, but in the meantime he's enjoying himself. He was born for this game, and he's been playing it since the day I was born, so he has twenty years' start on me. I'm not a person, it is not a smile of complicity he is putting on; it's a mask and an order, a way of gaining and wasting time while he's waiting for cards and bets. The doctor was a bit crazy, as ever, but he was right; there's a good few of us playing the same game. Everything now depends on how we play it. The old man and I both want money, and lots of it. We're also both weak enough to want it for its own sake, because we see it as the measure of a man. But he plays differently, and not just because of the size and number of the chips he has. To start with, he's not as desperate as me, although he has so little time left and knows it. Then again, he has the added advantage that, in all sincerity, what matters to him is the game and not what he stands to gain. For me too; he is my elder brother, my father, and I salute him. But I sometimes get frightened despite myself and want to know how it all adds up.

The woman and the man who had gone down the corridor hollowed out the distant silence with a soft, inhuman murmuring. Then there was the conclusive sound of a door pulled to, and the night of rain turned to one of pleasurable wind, no more real than a memory, beyond the shutters closed on to the square.

The stupor of the head leaning almost upright on the pillow, aware of the limits imposed by white, ferocious whiskers, drawing its strength from them, began to take on an impatient edge. Without much faith in the outcome, Larsen put on a great show of bowing his head, then drawing close as if to belatedly impart a secret. *I who spent so many nights pacing beneath these windows, my hand on my revolver or close to it, distant and uncaring, always with my useless challenge.*

He could hear a ship's horn repeated three times on the river; a weak, unconvincing, rasping sound. He felt for cigarettes, did not have the strength to undo the wet coat clinging to him, seducing him with its rank, cowardly smell, an odour of hangovers mingled with old fashioned hair lotions rubbed into his scalp in barbers' shops that parallel mirrors extended to infinity, shops probably long since demolished, certainly by now unbelievable. He suddenly suspected what everyone comes to understand sooner or later, that he was the only person alive in a world peopled by phantoms, that communication was impossible and not even desirable, that compassion was worth no more than hate, that a tolerant indifference, an attention divided between respect and sensuality, was all that could be asked for or be given.

"Yes, indeed," Petrus said, or perhaps only Petrus' voice. Then Larsen begged his pardon and explained in a few words that he was only acting out of a sense of loyalty and an uncontrollable, boundless identification with Jeremias Petrus and his plans. Rather than list them all, and with the modesty of an outsider who is guessing more than he knows, he gave a brief account of the dangers hidden in the forged certificate, creased by Galvez's hesitation between calculation and fear, and shown to Larsen in an absurd gesture of reckless defiance, a certificate he would no doubt continue to use, in a spirit of desperate irresponsibility that threatened to bring their world crashing down in a single, random moment.

Perhaps it was too late already. Of course, they could resort to violence and he, Larsen, personally guaranteed its success. But perhaps that green piece of paper, with the circular designs round the border, a number full of repetitions, and with Petrus' undeniable, swift, cramped signature bottom right, was not the only forged deed in circulation. In that case, violence would not only be useless but counterproductive.

Jeremias Petrus had listened with his eyes shut, or had shut them at a particular point in the story, a point Larsen was sorry he had missed. He lay slumped on the pillow, reduced to nothing more than this shrivelled head shamelessly displayed. His child's chest, his spindly legs, even his hands seemingly made out of bits of wire and old paper, hardly showed under the smooth covers. Nothing more than the blind, uncaring head, the mask prepared for a final shock, on the pillow. The wind showed no desire to approach; it was clearing the sky over the river, coming and going with mad tenacity, with an explanatory groan, with a wish to be rid of the trees and their leaves.

"That's how things stand," Larsen said in conclusion, annoyed with himself. "Perhaps it's not important, perhaps I was wrong. But Galvez is convinced the document is forged and that he can have you put in jail any morning he wakes up feeling queasy. Just imagine. I was at work in the General Manager's office, looking into a problem of metallisation, with that fellow shoving the crumpled green at me, as if he were letting me off lightly. I tried to ignore him, I showed him I didn't believe him. But I had to hire a fishing boat to come and see you, to warn you as soon as I could."

Petrus blinked, repeated "Yes, yes," several times with his eyes shut. Then he looked at Larsen, showing he had understood, instructing him that it was not necessary to bare his teeth or methodically and laboriously wrinkle up his face to form a smile. Yet Larsen knew that the impassive face was smiling and that the invisible but undeniable smile was one of greed and mockery which included him as well as Galvez, the share certificate, the danger, Petrus Ltd., and the destiny of mankind.

Petrus' eyes were open now, two narrow, watery spots of light beneath the black brows. He grudgingly explained that one of the certificates had been stolen right at the start of the minor foray into forgery, so unimportant but so vital to the great adventure he preferred to call an enterprise and had baptised with the name of Jeremias Petrus Ltd. To present the false document to the authorities could, he wearily conceded, cause further delays that would be all the more unfortunate as only days or at most weeks stood between him and victory or justice. Only one certificate was missing, that was the only danger. Larsen was covering the rearguard faithfully, and the urgency with which he had undertaken a journey by fishing boat on the stormy river was more than enough proof that he identified totally with the problems and risks of the enterprise. It was essential that the certificate should not reach the court in Santa Maria; any means of preventing this was valid and would be rewarded.

Petrus had closed his eyes again. It was obvious he wanted Larsen to go, that he was not really concerned whether the false deed was handed over or not. For the moment this was how he could enjoy himself, afterwards he would find something else. He had given up his belief in the spoils of the game many years earlier;

but as long as he lived he would go on believing, violently and joyously, in the game itself, in the agreed lie, in oblivion.

Feeling stirrings of envy, humbled by a confused admiration, Larsen tiptoed over to the stuccoed chimney to recover his hat, lumpy from the rain. He set it at its usual angle with two fingers and, still on tiptoe, walked back to the bed to stare down at Petrus from his full height, hands once more in his pockets.

Almost perpendicular to the blankets, the bald, white and yellow, black-browed mask seemed to be asleep; the thin defeated mouth was slackly shut. *There aren't many left like him. He wants me to get rid of Galvez for him, and the pregnant woman, and the pair of dogs. And he knows it's all for nothing. I'll say goodbye. If he wakes up and looks at me, I'll spit in his face.*

He leaned over without bending his knees and kissed Petrus on the forehead. The face remained still, safe in its absorption, secretive, yellow. Larsen straightened up, raised one finger to his hat brim. He tiptoed noiselessly across the dark sitting-room, reached the door and opened it; in the room at the end of the corridor, the man and woman who had gone past talking to each other were arguing furiously, the sound muffled by the wind, the wooden partitions, the distance.

SANTA MARIA III

If we are to believe the opinions and predictions of those who met Larsen and think they know him, everything points to the fact that after seeing Petrus he looked for and found the quickest possible means of returning to the shipyard.

He now needed — or simply had chosen to accept the need with all that was left of his rare, flickering enthusiasm — to lay hands on the forged share certificate, and to hand it back to Petrus in all modesty with nothing more than vague aims and curiosity, as if accomplishing a sacrifice from which he would gain no advantage beyond the complex vouchsafing of certain revelations.

Yet even though reason and the testimony of those who knew him might convince us that Larsen's only thought that night was to get back to the shipyard as soon as possible, in order to block any manoeuvre by the enemy he had just created for himself, to be on the spot to plan the rescue operation entrusted to him, it is also true that by this point in the story, no one is in any hurry, or if they are, their haste is of no importance.

Therefore, Larsen crossed to the far corner of the square, where he found himself standing in the wind and rain, realising to his astonishment, annoyance and irrepressible excitement, that the fact that the shipyard had become a complete, totally isolated and independent world, in no way precluded the existence of this other world, the one he was now immersed in, the one where he had once lived. He turned left and began to walk quickly parallel to the river, imagining he recognised street corners, damp house fronts and the strange glow cast by each infrequent street light, as it swung to and fro in the slackening drizzle.

After he had left the dark mass of the Customs house and its brightly-lit windows behind him, Larsen went down towards the river, on the road out to Enduro. The rain had ceased, and the wind was beginning to gust into the city, sweeping through one line of streets after another. *If I had to come back, why was it on a night like this, and why am I forcing myself towards the filthiest, most wretched part of the city?* He walked along, one hand clutching his coat lapels, head down to prevent the wind snatching away his hat, rainwater squelching in his socks at each resonant footfall.

By the time he could make out the dim yellow light of the café he could also smell the stench of dead fish. Half a block further on, he caught the strains of music, the scratchy rhythm of a waltz played on a guitar. He opened the door, then fumbled to close it behind him, as he stared at the smoke, the shadowy heads, the wretched-ness, the fleeting sense of comfort, the casual loathing, the always surprising features of the past. He walked up to the bar, a calculated air of challenge about him, concealing his emotion until he himself could fathom it.

"Don't you say hello to friends? I'm Barreiro, remember me?" From behind the counter, a young man smiled at him, his grubby white jacket buttoned to the neck, cheeks unshaven, a tired but lively expression on his face.

"Barreiro, of course," Larsen said, without the faintest idea of who he was talking to. He held out his hand, slapping the other's in greeting before shaking it warmly. They talked about the weather. Larsen ordered a rum. Making as though to lean on the bar, half turned towards the room, Larsen calmly, with no real curiosity, easily satisfied, looked over these people who had been his companions in this other world, at a time now dead and buried. The man in the centre of the room adjusted the guitar on his lap, his face beneath a wispy moustache wreathed in a smile. He tuned up while the others waited, impatient but with little respect, huddled against the weight and bluster of the wind. He recognised the sleepy, menacing expression on the faces of the half breed labourers, enticed to Enduro from farms or cattle ranches by some industrial fantasy of old man Petrus. The few women were stiff, gaudy, cheap. The guitar player rolled up his eyes, began another waltz. In a corner formed by the café's metal shutter, the backs of some wooden and tin signs, a huge iron hook, a spittoon full of dry, unidentifiable matter, and a sleeping black cat, a man and woman sat at a table clutching hands.

"They're saying again that the factory's going to close," Barreiro said. "But nobody ever knows why. There's more than enough fish to be had. It's hard to figure out what's wrong, especially for those poor fools who reckoned they could get rich on twenty or thirty pesos' pay. The one with the answers is Mr Big; he makes money when he closes and when he opens up again. Although you wouldn't think it. Are you back to stay? Not that I mean to pry."

"That's all right. Just passing through. I've got business in the north of the province."

"Business," Barreiro repeated, without the heart to smile.

Larsen looked at the tables and ran through some tango songs in his mind, independently of those the guitar was ruining, but which nevertheless lent meaning to the gestures, silences and the human traces in the faces hunched over their glasses. He shivered with cold, said yes to another rum. The man at the corner table had his head down, broad-shouldered in his check shirt, the side knot of the black kerchief round his neck visible. The woman's greasy hair hung over her eyes, and her repeated scowl of refusal was like a second face, a mobile but permanent mask which she only cast off, perhaps, when she slept. And everything that Larsen dredged up and reconstructed from experience, with the help of intuitions that had in the past proved accurate, was not enough to convince him that beneath the clumsy signs of tenderness, rejection, modesty and pathetic vanity that seeped like a patina through her quivering skin, there really still existed the woman's original face, the one she had been born with, not made or helped to make.

Nobody has ever seen that face, if it does exist. Because she can only wear it, show it unadorned, when she is alone, when there is no mirror or filthy window-pane nearby for her to glance or squint at herself in. The worst of it is – and it's not just her I'm thinking of – that if by some miracle, surprise or act of betrayal she did get the chance to see the face she has been busy concealing since she was thirteen, there is no way she could like or even recognise it. But she at least will enjoy the privilege of dying more or less young, before wrinkles make another, final mask, far harder to remove than this one. Then perhaps, with her face at peace, cleansed of the sad, restless worry of living, she will be fortunate enough to have two old women strip her bare, pass comment on her, wash her, then dress her again. Nor is it beyond the bounds of possibility that a few of those who drop into her hovel for a farewell drink will shake over her, standing stiff and formal, a sprig soaked in holy water, and watch the odd crystal shape the droplets briefly form in the capricious candlelight. And if that happens, I suppose it can be said that someone will finally have seen her face, and her life will not have been in vain.

Cajoling, pleading, the man in the check shirt reached out to the wavering mask. Outside and above, oblivious to men cowering in their corners, the wind howled, roaring as it pressed down on crops, trees, the shiny nocturnal flanks of cattle. The guitar-player was starting another song, rising half out of his seat to thank someone for buying him a drink. Barreiro saw Larsen staring at the woman.

"Would you credit her?" he said, admiration mingling with contempt in his voice. "She's capable of arguing over the price all night. They call her the Northerner — perhaps she's from where you're headed. She's a tough one, all right. But a good friend apart from that."

The wind gusted playfully over the café roof, the straight dirt streets, the canning factory, its full force now aimed at la Colonia, the fields of winter wheat, the milk train chugging its way across the black plain out beyond the city.

"When is the next ferry up-river?" Larsen asked, turning back to the counter. He felt in his pockets as if he wanted to pay. "Please, it's on me," Barreiro said. "The ferries don't start until six. But perhaps there'll be a cargo boat willing to take you."

The man had eased his broad, check-patterned back against the chair. Now that the price had been fixed, the woman stopped pulling faces and contented herself with a smile in which malicious reproach combined with a savouring of secret pleasures, a smile she could maintain throughout their walk to her room, if need be until dawn. The man ordered two drinks to celebrate.

So the world, this one, the one to which all the others still belonged, had not changed, was not affected by his desertion. Larsen said goodbye to the man who claimed to be Barreiro and headed across the room, adopting out of respect the roll, the world-weary disdain with which he had crossed so many filthy café floors during his long, ever so remote, residence on this other planet.

Larsen had his first real glimpse of awareness as he sat huddled on the boat, his hands clutching the ticket stretched out towards the imprecise little waves formed and spread by the ship's prow. A newly-born sun was trying out its apathetic, piercing clarity. *A morning; a bright, fresh winter's morning,* Larsen thought, to take his mind off the idea. Then, since there can be no courage without forgetfulness: *This winter light on a windless day that's bound up in its indifferent chill gaze is enveloping me, is looking at me. I will carry out, as indifferent as the white light shining on to me, the first, the second, then the third action, and so on until I have to stop, satisfied or*

*exhausted, and admit that something incomprehensible, useful perhaps
for someone else, has been accomplished through me.*

A mile further on he yawned, firmly pushed back the black,
protective hat. He surveyed the sleepy, tremulous bodies lolling
beside him on the ferry's horseshoe-shaped bench. He blinked and
turned his smarting eyes to the new day, blind, irrepressible, the
same day whose light had slid over the stupor of the giant scaly
haunches and would again slide, with equally unexpected precision, over herds of other beasts born of man's renewed absence.

It was at that moment — the ferry turned to bob its way to the
rotten landing stage known as "The Portuguese Place" — that
Larsen allowed himself, like someone deliberately fingering a sore,
to give way to the outriders of fear, to apostasy, to accessible terror
which was diminished, bearable only because it had become
blunted in its long siege of him, because it had been infected with a
human quality. He thought: *This body; legs, arms, sex, guts, all that
allows me to be acquainted with people and things; the head, which is me
and therefore cannot exist for me; but also the hollow of my chest, which is
not hollow but is filled with scraps, shavings and scrapings, dust, the
remains of everyone once dear to me, everything which in the other world I
allowed to make me happy or sad. And all of it so much at ease there,
always ready for anything, if I had permitted myself to stay there, or had
been able to.* .

SANTA MARIA IV

The reddish sun was already high over the river. It was time for Dr Diaz Grey to wake up, to grope for his first cigarette, his eyes still shut tight trying to save what he could of the images of his dream, to buttress their sense of nostalgia and sweetness without fresh encroachments. A mother, a long-forgotten girlfriend, a smile peering down at his pillow — or the ephemeral whiteness of some farewell — at the face more entirely his, the purer, slightly younger face that he imagined himself to possess when asleep.

He lit his cigarette; half opened his eyes in the darkened room, gingerly gauging the heat and temperature of the day he had just been plunged into. He thought of his sick visits, visits by the sick, of the good and bad points of solitude, of the previous evening's conversation with Larsen, of Petrus' daughter. He had only really met her twice.

For years the Petrus family lived in Santa Maria, Puerto Astillero, and various European cities, without spending more than a few months in any one place. Old man Petrus naturally spent less time away than the rest of whichever family group was travelling. In fact, he did little more than accompany his wife and daughter, a governess, a sister-in-law or sister, install them safely and comfortably, leave their lives planned for a while down to the last detail, only to enable himself to forget them without remorse, with a joyful, anticipated calculation. He was a small, dry man, rapid and precise in his movements, with stiff sidewhiskers that in those days were black. He wore bowler hats and the tight-fitting suits with short jackets that were typical of the post-war years, a fashion that seemed specifically invented for his kind of complex, austere dignity. There were still surprising echoes of that fashion in the clothes he ordered nowadays. He seemed more like a servant, a butler, a family adviser whose only reward was the satisfaction of seeing a job well done rather than a husband or father; unconcerned about receiving thanks, not interested whether the wife (the daughter had not yet been born or did not count) and the inevitable relative (different on each journey, but always the same) agreed with his ideas about comfort, standing, salubriousness or the beauty of the view.

He was determined to achieve these small triumphs of organisation not so much out of vanity, which quite probably never needed any outside stimulus, but because he must have considered this success as the gentle, stimulating exercise of his powers at times when his business affairs were necessarily no more than fears and fantasies. Those tiny, useful, negligible triumphs scored with and against train timetables, tourist brochures, road maps, guides and friendly advice.

Eventually, with the 1930 crisis, the family settled in Puerto Astillero: for ever in the case of señora Petrus, who was buried in the La Colonia cemetery after twenty-four hours of wrangling. Petrus was set on keeping the body, the worms' breeding ground, the skeleton and the ashes in his own garden, in a small, sloping-roofed construction of marble and iron which the builder Ferrari hastily designed and even managed to get some payment for. And after swearing a solemn oath in the presence of the mourners, a priest and the gravediggers, an oath whose dramatic, violent hyperboles were doubtless provoked by his defeat at the hands of functionaries and municipal byelaws, Petrus finally accepted that she be buried in the cemetery at La Colonia. There was also a telegram sent to the governor, three lines so imperious in tone they ought to have been signed "I, Petrus". This produced no reply beyond a letter of condolence in which the expressions of sympathy were designed to counterbalance a refusal to do anything at all, and which in any case arrived after a week's rain had fallen on señora Petrus' tomb in La Colonia. (It was in winter she died; Angelica Ines was incapable of forgetting it).

After an oath sworn in German which in the last resort could only exclude the few native-born people who formed part of the cortege of muddy mourners: "As God is my Witness, I Swear that your Body will Rest in Peace in our Fatherland". Capitals for emphasis. A gesture hard to understand. None of the evidence about Petrus leads one to expect this melodramatic, haughty, hatless man drawn to his full height, arm raised above the muddy pit as he pronounced the barbaric, guttural words of an oath that was never fulfilled. Afterwards, he shrank back, accepted the handful of earth he was offered, and let it fall on top of the three intertwined letters on the purple ribbon draped round the coffin.

Before that, in the house of mourning, scarcely an hour after her death, Ferrari the builder, obsequiously scribbling on white paper, desperately keen to understand and to prove his fidelity, had calculated the cost of the marble, the wrought iron, the wages of the bricklayers and marble craftsmen, the cost of the freight. Yet he found himself also somehow in the grip of the pleasure and anguish of the artist, struggling to create and interpret. Petrus the widower paced up and down behind him, stubborn, insistent, constantly fussing, impossible to please.

Perhaps Petrus and his daughter had also decided to stay for ever in the house at Puerto Astillero. They added bedrooms, had statues brought for the garden, and for weeks the river boats earned their hire transporting crates full of furniture, crockery and ornaments.

But before they settled in their house on its fourteeen pillars, defence against a flood the like of which has never been seen on the river, there was Petrus' attempt to buy the Latorre palace, on an island near the port of Santa Maria. His meetings with the fat, soft, degenerate descendants of the national hero are worthy of being recorded and distorted. He flattered, schemed, forbore and, it seems, succeeded in offering enough money to reach a preliminary agreement with them. He would have had as residence — on the island that the boats entering and leaving the bay have to round at a respectful distance — the palace with pink, everlastingly dank walls, a hundred iron-barred windows, and its round tower which once upon a time must have seemed a daring, scarcely believable feat of architecture.

Perhaps that, Petrus on his island, would have changed his story and ours; perhaps fate, as easily impressed as crowds are by pomp and splendour, would have decided to help him, would have accepted the aesthetic or harmonious need to safeguard the future of the legend; Jeremias Petrus, emperor of Santa Maria, Enduro and Puerto Astillero. Petrus, our lord and master, watching over us, our needs and our wages from the palace's round tower. Perhaps Petrus would have had a lighthouse built on the top; or maybe it would have been enough for us on fine nights, to adorn and enliven our servitude, to stand on the river promenade and gaze at its windows blazing so brightly they looked like stars, while inside Jeremias Petrus burnt the midnight oil governing our destinies. But just at the moment when the hero's grandchildren, amused or disgusted at Petrus' ability to covet, implicate, forget snubs, haggle, and then deliver at the end of each meeting, in his soft, mellow voice, with his face from another century, a ruthless resumé of all that had been discussed and offhandedly accepted, were slowly nodding their heads in agreement, just then it was decided, in the face of destiny, to declare the Latorre palace a national monument. The nation was to buy it and pay a supply teacher in national history to live there and send regular reports on any leaks, threats from weeds, the relation between tides and the state of its foundations. The teacher's name, of no importance here, was Aranzuru. He was said to have been a lawyer, but was not one now.

Diaz Grey had only really met Petrus' daughter twice. The first time was after they moved into the house in Puerto Astillero and before her mother died. The girl, who must have been about five year old, got a fish-hook stuck in her leg. Doubtless if Petrus had been at home he would have driven the child beyond Santa Maria to the clinic in La Colonia, preferring her to lose more blood, forgetting there was a doctor's plaque in the new square and deaf to all attempts to remind him. But the old man, that is, the Petrus of those days, the same as now but with black, stiffer sidewhiskers, must have been doing sums in the capital in between meetings of probable shareholders, or was away in Europe buying machinery, contracting technicians. So it was the mother or the aunt on duty who had to face the situation and the possible outcomes: death, lameness, Petrus' vengeful fury. "Just think, doctor, her father always forbade her to go on to the fishermen's pier." The old man called it a pier, even though at that time it was nothing more than a platform on top of a mud wall (but the blocks of stone had already begun to make their way up-river). It is likely that he wrote the word pier when he scribbled down the first plan for the place, or thought "pier" when he first came ashore, with a disdainful sneer, to examine the spot and buy it. As for fishermen, there was only Poetters, who later became owner of the Belgrano, but who in those days lived on his own in a shack on the riverbank, because of a wager or a quarrel with his father or because of both.

The little girl, her maid and the dog had nothing better to do while the others were sleeping their siesta than to cluster round the immobile Poetters and improve his chances of catching something with their own concerns. Poetters made to cast his line, heard the strange noise — more like a warning shout than a cry of pain —

and scarcely bothered to stoop over the girl's leg, knowing he would be too scared to do anything about it. He sent the maid to tell them up at the house, cut the line next to the hook, then disappeared with his rod, the tin of bait, and all his primitive tackle of sticks, lead weights, wires and floats.

They found her lying there, making no sound, comforted by the dog's timid licking. No one, not the mother or the aunt, or anyone from the battery of servants, gardeners and others with uncertain functions who came running out of the house (finished two years earlier, but still undergoing improvements), or any soldier from the other, less committed regiment of building workers (or perhaps these were carpenters too by now) constructing the shipyard and at that moment having lunch in the midst of the vague geometric shapes of beams and bricks — no one dared pull out the hook, which was stuck in the back of the girl's thigh, close to her buttock.

Once she had recovered from her terror at being surrounded by so many faces showing fear or offering advice, a smile returned to Angelica Ines' face. She sank back into her mystery, sturdy, sunburnt, blinking her big bright unquestioning eyes, shaking the stiff, rope-like braids of her hair in the breezeless afternoon air. Diaz Grey could imagine her, the water used to wash the wound drying on her leg, luminous in the light of the siesta hour; the thin scrawl of dark red blood continually seeping out: invulnerable and in reality intact; the silvery half anchor of the fish-hook become part of her, incorporated into her body and her placidity.

Pushed this way and that by pleas and warnings, aware of their responsibility, rehearsing the panic they would have to overcome when faced with Petrus' black beetling eyebrows, with his explosion of insults or his silence, the mother or the aunt put their trust in God and made a choice. They bound her leg with a silk handkerchief, then mother and aunt, with the foreman from the shipyard building at the wheel, drove the girl to Santa Maria along the ill-defined dirt road.

A newcomer to the town, Diaz Grey was impervious to the growing prestige of Petrus' name, repeated to him as a promise, a magic password or a threat, and put up with that strange kind of hysteria they filled his surgery with and which after a few months practising in La Colonia would come to seem to him the most normal, everyday, predictable hysteria imaginable.

The girl on the couch, her round face staring blankly up at the ceiling, calmly absorbing the hook. The two dowdily dressed women, in their large flat shoes, with big bosoms and thick, luxuriant hair, like thoroughbred animals, oblivious to their own presence, only taking from the world the tiny portion they cared about, lurched between urgent voices of tragedy, explanations and the muffled sobs of choked back tears, and silent retreats from the couch which ended with their broad backs, their curved haunches flattened against the walls. They stood there panting, full of ghastly awareness, before they plunged back into the fray. And the European foreman, who with a curt shake of the head had refused to stay in the waiting room, leant silent in the doorway, sweatily proud of his loyalty.

Diaz Grey gave her an anaesthetic, made an incision, offered the mother (or aunt) the S-shaped hook as a souvenir. Her grey, glassy eyes stared up at the gentle glow from the ceiling or on the movements of the doctor's head, Angelica Ines let herself be injected, cut, wrapped in bandages. She did not say a word. Her round suntanned face expressed nothing more, above the tight tresses of her hair on the couch, than her never frustrated habit of waiting for someone else to act, or for the feeling which was bound to replace previous ones, its daughter and executioner, without pause, without being able to stop, because long before stretching out on his couch for the first time she had dismissed death once and for all.

The second occasion — by that time Diaz Grey knew all about the meaning of the name Petrus, but was not intimidated — was not really a memory any more. Perhaps the lived experience was forgotten and gone, and in its place was (motionless, accurate, whimsically coloured) the memory of a cheap print that the doctor had never seen and that no one had ever painted. The irreality, the feeling that the scene had taken place or been recorded a hundred years earlier, was the product, almost uncertainly, of the softness, the ochre tones of the light it bathed in.

Old man Petrus was standing drawn up to full height in the foreground, allowing his whiskers to turn from grey to white, not exactly smiling but hinting unofficially, indulgently, that he was capable of smiling, his eyes chill and piercing, his left hand holding the cigar he had just lit against his waistcoat, its aroma as intrinsic to the print as the geometric planes of the shifting yellows which illuminated the scene.

A child could have cut out the figure of Petrus and stuck it in an album: then everyone would have believed the old man was posing for a portrait, alone, with no other details but the curved back of the wooden chair he was pretending to rest his right hand on, with a background of plates hanging on the walls and beer mugs on the mantelpiece. To Petrus' right, the light shining on little more than the tip of a bonnet, the gentle swell of a cheek, their strong round knees, the mother or an aunt sat knitting. Diaz Grey had forgotten exactly when Petrus lost his wife. Behind Petrus to the left, two shadowy women with hypocritical, flustered faces hovered around the huge uncomfortable armchair where Angelica Ines, expecting nothing, sat smiling through her sweat, her legs wrapped in a hide blanket, her heavy square jaw thrust forward in a vague, un- threatening way. The fire flamed silently behind Petrus. It was a still, warm autumn afternoon, in the print also.

The girl, who must have been about fifteen, had fainted at lunch when she discovered a worm in a pear. Now she was rocking from side to side in the armchair, her broad blank face turned mysteriously to the ceiling, a trickle of saliva dribbling from her mouth, sweat beading her upper lip, her plaits thicker by now, their tips no longer pointing upwards.

All at once Petrus informed Diaz Grey that the same car which had brought him from Santa Maria was at his disposal to take him back. On the steps Petrus took his arm — neither as a friend, nor putting pressure on him, above the sleeping garden with its slightly confused symmetry, its thick, dark greens, beginning to be populated with white statues — and stopped to take in the evening and the shipyard building with an impartial pride, as if he were responsible for both.

"I'll make sure you receive your fee, doctor." So Diaz Grey realised that he was not being paid on the spot, out of consideration for his feelings, and to separate the health of Petrus' daughter from any idea of monetary gain; but also so he should not forget that his time and skill were things that Petrus could buy. "My daughter, doctor, is perfectly normal. I could show you diagnoses signed by the most eminent physicians of Europe. Professors."

"There's no need," Diaz Grey said, freeing himself gently from the hand on his arm. "I came to examine her because of her slight accident. And that slight accident is in no way abnormal."

"That's right," Petrus agreed. "Normal, perfectly normal, as far as you and the whole town are concerned, doctor. The whole world, for that matter."

Diaz Grey stroked the dog sniffing at his shoes and took a step down.

"Quite," he said, looking back. "It's not only in Europe that doctors take an oath when they graduate. And not only professors."

Petrus waved the cigar in front of him and bowed ceremoniously, heels together. "I'll make sure you receive your fee," he repeated.

Those had been the only two occasions. There were other times when Diaz Grey had caught glimpses of the Petrus girl coming out of Mass in Santa Maria or when, a grown woman since that afternoon of the worm and the fainting fit, she was in town doing some shopping, accompanied first by an aunt, then later by Josefina, who became her maid after the family had finally settled in Puerto Astillero.

Seen like that, in the distance, she seemed to bear out all the diagnoses old man Petrus had collected. She was tall, plump, with a large bosom and hips that could not be concealed by the wide dark bell-shaped skirts she wore for years from a pattern chosen and cut by a zealous maiden aunt. Her skin was very white, and her bright grey eyes seemed incapable of looking to the sides without the aid of her slow, thick neck; she always wore her hair in braids, twisted round her head as she grew older.

Someone said she was prone to sudden, uncontrollable fits of laughter. Diaz Grey had never seen her laugh. So out of all that her heavy body could have shown or confessed to him as she made her way through the narrow confines of the town in the wake of relatives, a rare friend, or her maid, the only thing which attracted his dormant professional curiosity was her slow, laboured, falsely stately walk.

He was never really sure what memory this sight awoke in him. Angelica Ines moved her feet forward cautiously, not raising one from the ground until she was sure the other was firmly planted, with the toes turned slightly inwards, or perhaps only giving that impression. Always drawn to her full height, she seemed to be leaning back into her previous step, a gesture that accentuated the roundness of her breasts and stomach. As if she were continually walking down a hilly street, and was adjusting her body to maintain her poise without breaking into a run, Diaz Grey had thought at first. But it was not exactly that, or there was something more. One noonday the word processional came to him, and seemed closer to the truth. Hers was a processional step, or was from that moment on; it was as though she was advancing, scarcely swaying, despite being held back by the twin impediments of the slow pace demanded by a religious procession and the sheer weight of the invisible symbol she was carrying — a cross, a huge candle, a canopy pole.

THE SHIPYARD V

Cursing the cold, determined not to think of anything else, Larsen went straight to the office building from the embarkation.

It was a clear morning, grey and blue; the peaceful light shone down calmly, watchful, not in the least impatient. The puddles scooped in the mud were still transparent, glistening from their covering of ice; the sparse trees gleamed dark and sodden in distant gardens. Larsen halted, tried to understand the meaning of the landscape around him, listened to the silence. *It's fear*. But he had lost all concern; it was like the nagging, gentle, companionable pain of a chronic illness, one you are not going to die of, because it is only possible to die with it.

He looked back at the still, dirty river and then violently shook the keys on the key-ring bulging in his hip pocket, the ridiculous, childish abundance of keys that symbolised importance, power and possession. He opened the doors one by one, choosing the right key at a single glance, twisting his wrist with a precise gesture; the iron entry gate, hard to shift, almost convincing, the stairway door which led to the various departments, then up on the first floor, amid all the grimy, frozen solitude, the door to his own office. Doors without glass or wooden panels, with fake locks, which burst open at the slightest blow or puff of wind, but which Galvez, cheerfully obstinate, flashing his teeth at nothing, contrived to lock each evening and re-open every morning.

Larsen sat now in the General Manager's office, leaning back behind his desk, his shoulders and the flexible chair spine pressed against the wall. He was relaxing, not from the bad night he had spent or the things he had done in it, but from things themselves, from the as yet unknown actions he was about to begin to perform, one after the other, without passion, as if he were merely lending his body to them. Hands behind his head, his black hat tilted over one eye, he mentally checked off the tasks he had accomplished that winter, as though to convince an indifferent witness that the bare room could really be taken for the General Manager's office of a prosperous, thriving company. The hinges and the lettering on the door, the bits of cardboard in the windows, the patched up linoleum, the files in alphabetical order, the dusted emptiness of his desk, the buzzers in perfect working order for calling the staff. And, beyond the visible and demonstrable but just as essential, the hours of work and absorbed thought he had put in at the office, his unflinching determination to create in his mind a phantom legion of workers and employees.

He could also cite in his defence, it seemed to him in this idle, pointless process of self-justification, something which apparently belied it: those evenings when a truck parked at the back of the shipyard, the slow, professionally indifferent and suspicious pair of men who walked to the centre of the waste ground between the office building and the main shed, opposite the cabin where Galvez and his woman lived. They met up with Galvez and Kunz, and sometimes he himself was there to watch them talk, to witness the methodical bargaining with an unchanging air of censure and disdain, as though he were a judge rather than an accomplice.

The group greeted each other, four or five hands raised to the side of the head, then they set off across the mud to the shed door, whose dark shadow swallowed them up. The visitors chose without enthusiasm, without anyone urging them. Kunz dragged out into the light that shone vertically through the broken roof some object or other, which had not been asked for, merely mentioned in a questioning, derogatory way. The men from the truck sauntered over to inspect it, frowned and pointed out to each other laconically, almost moved to compassion, the ravages of rust, how out-of-date it was, the huge gap between what they were looking for and what they were being offered.

Perched on a heap of scrap metal, Galvez watched them, teeth bared, nodding. When the men made as if to finish their infinite list of objections, Kunz leaned nonchalantly on the article for sale and proceeded to extol its virtues, the quality of its steel, its technical superiority, just why it was suited to not only their needs but any other possible needs or interest in the whole wide world. Always in the background, a metre outside the circle around the object, Larsen stared at Kunz's expressionless face as he spoke in his accented monotone, filling the static, slatey air of the shed with his lies, as if he were tired of enumerating its obvious characteristics, as if he were giving a class at a technical school, with no more interest or hope beyond that of making himself understood. Kunz finished his talk, closed the hand he had been resting on the object, then stepped back from it, the circle, the bargaining. A silence followed, sometimes interrupted by the dogs or the wind; the men from the truck exchanged glances without speaking, smiled pityingly and shook their heads.

Then it was Galvez's turn. They all knew it, even if they refused to look at him. Galvez knew he was master of the silence, let it spread and spread. The two men in overalls a metre from the object, as motionless and stiff as it was; Kunz invisible, propped against the wall shelving, separated from the scene by years and kilometres; Larsen too perhaps, apathetic, wearing his thick black overcoat and his hat, the nervous tic of his mouth conveying contempt, inexhaustible patience. Although no one moved, the centre of the circle shifted from the object to Galvez's bald patch, to his smile. Finally he began to speak, setting his trap:

"Tell us for a start whether you're interested or not. Just as it is, as useless as you were saying it was. You asked for a perforator, and here it is. It may not be brand-new, but it's not worthless either. According to the inventory, even after depreciation, it's worth five thousand six hundred. Say yes or no, we've got a lot to do. Make an offer. Even if it's only to give us a laugh."

At this point, one of the men spoke up; the other agreed. His long teeth bared, as if they were his whole face, or at least the only part of it capable of expressing anything and of being understood, Galvez waited for the figure which fluttered at the end of a long hesitant phrase before falling, harsh and heavy. He would do them the favour of hearing him laugh, stated his final price (twenty per cent above what he was willing to accept) and sat stolidly until the buyers, complaining and proffering tame insults, raised their initial offer to the level he had in mind. While this was going on, the visitors spoke without looking at each other or at anything other than the object itself, as though they were bargaining with among themselves.

Once they had talked themselves up to his price, Galvez stood up, produced a book of receipts and a pen, walked yawning over to the object shining dully in the light from the hole in the roof.

"I never haggle. Cash in hand. The purchaser pays transport."

The three of them shared out the banknotes and never mentioned the matter again. The same thing happened once or twice a month. But he, Larsen, had never allowed himself to be implicated in these thefts from Petrus or the company; he had merely received his share, he had looked on with silent rancour while the unchanging rite took place, always refusing to lend a hand to load what had been bought on to the truck.

When he heard Kunz and Galvez arrive at nine o'clock on that cold, bright morning he took off his hat and coat, waited until the sounds of their arrival had died down, then summoned them with their unmistakable buzzers. First he called nobody; then again, nobody: first the Technical Manager and then the Administrative Manager. He did not ask them to sit down, but started to explain, with calculated slowness, exaggerating the glances, the enthusiasm and the pauses, that Petrus was in Santa Maria, that the judge had lifted the embargo on the shipyard, and that the promised or forecast days of power and glory were about to dawn. He realised they did not believe him and did not care; perhaps that was what he wanted. Around noon he went down to the shed, openly carrying a briefcase. He stole an ammeter. On his way back he greeted Galvez's woman, out gathering wood for her fire. She straightened up to smile at him, in the man's coat, her belly apparently about to burst in the taut, blue air of the late morning. Poetters, the owner of the Belgrano, had a friend interested in ammeters. Larsen took four hundred pesos for it, left two hundred to settle debts. He ate there, and over his cup of coffee was planning a visit to Petrus' house, a meeting that evening with Angelica Ines, first in the summerhouse then in the house, where he had still never set foot, an incursion that would end with their engagement, blessed by Petrus himself, who would have arrived before nightfall by boat or car.

But Angelica Ines beat him to it. Between four and five that afternoon, while Larsen was in his manager's office examining a musty typewritten report signed by an earlier, unidentifiable General Manager, recommending the sale of all the company's assets to raise money to fit out a small fishing fleet, the Technical Manager Kunz tapped on his door and came in, a smile of apprehension and anticipated nostalgia on his face, with only the faintest, inevitable trace of mockery.

"Excuse me, there's a young lady who wishes to see you. And it doesn't matter whether you agree or not, she'll see you anyway.

119

Galvez is trying to head her off, but he'll not succeed. Shall I show her in, or let her push her way past?"

Kunz was standing beside the desk, his smile now merely nostalgic in the midst of the silver bristles of his stubble. The door was flung open and the woman came to a halt inside the office, paused for breath, laughed a brief laugh that was over almost before it began.

This part of the story is written out of a sense of loyalty to a ghost. There is no proof that it is true; and everything points to its being improbable. But Kunz swore he saw and heard it. Months later, all the maid would admit was that "her mistress's dress was a bit untidy". Kunz closed the General Manager's door and went back to his desk, leaving the woman with Larsen. He winked at Galvez, who was sitting, elbows on some unopened account books he had brought over from the filing cabinet, gazing up at the blue sky through a hole. Kunz sat down and began to pore over his stamp album.

According to Kunz, they did not have time to do much. Before the screams, they could hear Larsen's voice, going through a persuasive, painful defence; although he was talking softly, and obviously trying to keep his voice down, he did not seem to be speaking to the girl alone; it was easy to imagine him standing there, five fingertips resting on the desktop, a pained expression on his face, a boundless reserve of tolerance, listing for a dozen Galvezes or Kunzes the benefits to be gained from patience, the compensations reserved for those who have faith and wait. Like old man Petrus at one of the meetings he had tricked the shareholders into attending, boring them stiff until they were ready to sign away anything if only they were left in peace.

But Larsen needed a breathing space, or to find arguments the girl might understand. There was complete silence in the General Manager's office, broken only by the sound (or at least Kunz had imagined he heard it) of Galvez chewing his fingernails, and the remote, muffled but jagged reverberations of a winter's evening on river and field. Then both of them began to shout: her voice strangely pure, as if she were singing, Larsen repeating over and over:

"I swear to you by all that's holy."

Her voice, reappearing like a musical motif in the argument, like a silver fish leaping, somersaulting in the air, as Kunz heard her say, or swore on oath he had:

"With that slut. That filthy slut."

Then she screamed, as she opened the door: "Don't touch me. Look."

Beyond a doubt, Larsen had only wanted to keep her there, or to settle their skirmish with a tender gesture. Or to cover her up. For immediately afterwards, in Kunz's unverifiable version that disqualified Galvez as a witness because he, absurdly, "spent the whole time staring out through the broken window and chewing his nails, giving no indication that he had heard or noticed anything", the girl Angelica Ines came out of the general manager's office quickly though not at a run; head held high and body tilted back, bumping against the peeling wall as she crossed the vast expanse of the room, past its few pieces of furniture and the two hunched men, past the clearer lines on the floor where lengths of partition, long since burnt for firewood, had once stood.

"She crossed the whole ruin without seeing it, just as she had not given it a look when she arrived. She was always dressed up as a little girl, by her mother, her aunt, by habit; but that afternoon she was dressed as a woman, in a long black dress through which her underwear, a slip or something, was visible, and incredibly high heeled shoes which she had borrowed or was wearing for the first time and which must have got ruined on her way home. Because she came, they came, on foot from the house to the yard. Shoes which, if you had not seen her walk without heels, would have seemed to explain her strange way of walking, like a fat or pregnant woman trying to keep her balance. But the important part, the part I was holding back and would like to delay still longer if I knew how to without being boring, was that the bodice of her dress was undone, not torn but hanging open. I'll try to explain. She teetered over the rotten wooden floor, over puddles, blueprints, business letters, the stains left by rain and time. Cutting through the fetid air of winter, the braids of her fair hair tilted up not provocatively, but simply unaware of it all, the faint gleam of a dazed smile on her lips, oblivious to us, to the smell of rats and failure. Beyond her, wringing his hands behind the door to his office, too afraid to show himself or to say anything out of fear that Galvez or I would hear him, a rogue, a fat, dirty, old man at his wits' end. All that, if you get me, and so many other things it would take too long . . . that's why I was so slow. But it is useless, or almost, to try to explain to anyone who was not there and did not see and does not know who she was and who he was, what the shipyard was like, or even who I am, born in this country but with revalidated European papers, living there then, like that. So try to imagine, and this is the easy part, a well-built young woman walking rapidly but without running along the wall of an endless, almost deserted office, displaying the most perfect pair of breasts ever. And it was not that poor devil Larsen who had torn off her bodice, but she herself who had undone it, without pulling off a button or ripping the tulle. I followed her with my gaze until she reached the top of the stairs, and there was the maid waiting for her with a coat that she reached out for and slipped round round her shoulders; and I think that Angelica Ines slapped her, as if it had been the maid who had put her up to it, who had dressed her and brought her there and now, maternal and wanting to avoid a scandal, was leading her tamely away. And the woman, the filthy slut she had been shouting about could have been none other, as far as I can tell, and now there is no risk in saying it, none other than Galvez's woman, who must have been in the ninth month of pregnancy, as we were soon to discover."

That, essentially, is Kunz's version of what happened, related by him, without any suspicious amendments, to Father Favieri and to Dr Diaz Grey. But the doctor does not believe it; his incredulity is based on his acquaintance with Angelica Ines some years later. Nor does he believe that Kunz, who may be still alive and may read this book, was deliberately lying. It is possible that Kunz interpreted Angelica Ines' visit to the shipyard as having solely a sexual motive; it is possible that his solitary existence, his daily encounters with Galvez's woman (who was unavailable at the time), made him prone to that sort of hallucination; it is also possible that he was deluded in retrospect when he saw the maid covering the young woman with her coat, and imagined she was protecting her from shame rather than simply from the cold.

THE CABIN V

Yet in essence Larsen's undeniable decline was the decline of what was already there, not any real change. Years earlier he would have been keener, more cunning, in his pursuit of the two women he thought of as "the crazy one" and "the pregnant one". But he would have done exactly the same thing. Nor would the young Larsen have tried to reach old man Petrus before he could place the forged certificate he had promised to recover on his desk or in his hands. It is also beyond dispute that the young Larsen, whom nobody could now accurately discern, would have behaved just as his older self was doing, and contented himself with recapturing and tortuously preserving a romantic, false prestige in the garden blanched by statues, in the summerhouse pierced alike by the cold and the barking of the dog, in the unbreakable silences he had lapsed back into forever. And that same young Larsen, more eagerly and spontaneously, with less falsity and infinitely less repugnance, would have helped the woman in the overcoat, Galvez's woman, the woman with the silky, plump dogs, to fetch water, make the fire, clean the meat and peel the potatoes.

Finally freed from his tight overcoat and his hat, not that bald all things considered, a lock of grey hair slanting down his forehead as he leaned over the steaming pots, wielding the knife with a steady sureness. Identical in all the basics, this Larsen who could have been the other's son. The only difference being that the young Larsen was more impatient, whereas this Larsen who squatted down to talk in the corner of the cabin that served as kitchen was a better dissembler.

This only lasted a few days. He helped her cook, played with the dogs, chopped wood, demonstrated that his heavy round buttocks had chosen this spot once and for all, this smoky, warm corner. He peeled potatoes assiduously, recommended seasonings. He stared at the woman's belly to reassure himself that disgust would keep him from any surrender or weakness. When alone with her, he never paid her any compliment her husband had not heard. He became cheerful and talkative, an ally of stupidity, soft and sentimental. He deliberately gave the impression of being exhausted, exaggerating his old age.

No, he did not have to wait long, though he, Larsen, was prepared to wait a hundred years or, at least, to forget that he was waiting. Heavy but agile, eager to please, sure of arousing sympathy, lavishly dispensing (because he would never again have need of it) all the false, nauseous kindness he had been soaking up without difficulty or hindrance over long years of exploiting and suffering women.

That was in the last days of July, when winter has already become a habit and its gentle stimulus, the strange way it isolates and magnifies people and things, has become almost enjoyable. There is still a long time before it grows loathsome, before the first invisible buds fill us with impatience as they become the sworn enemies of the frost and the heavy-bellied clouds, the exiled, nostalgic sons of an long-awaited spring.

Larsen was nearly always alone with the woman in the evenings, because Galvez, who rarely smiled now, left the cabin as soon as he had eaten, or did not even bother to eat there. Stripped of its smile, his face had an alien, lifeless look, ghastly in its lack of shame; freed from the reflection of its white mask, it bore witness to, flaunted, solitude, self-absorption, an obscene indifference. Occasionally Kunz stayed on, disturbing the dogs' sleep by trying to teach them to walk on their hind legs, but he was no more than an accomplice ready for anything, for whatever might come to pass, for an act not yet formulated. The cold weather flaked his fair skin and brought out his foreign accent.

The woman and Larsen had come at last to talk about the forged certificate.

"I can't ask Galvez for it. I don't wish to offend, señora, but you know he won't listen to reason. That's how he is. One of these days he'll take leave of his senses and present it to the court. Perhaps that'll make him happy, though I doubt it. What worries me is to have to run the risk. What if he presents the certificate and they arrest Petrus? Do you know what the creditors committee is? A conglomerate, in a word. It's not fifteen or twenty individuals, it's simply a conglomerate which for the moment allows us to live in peace because it has forgotten us, forgotten the shipyard, the failure of the business, the money thrown away. But as soon as the judge signs the arrest warrant, they'll start to remember. They won't be content simply to say, 'It's too bad Petrus got us involved in this mess, he thought it was a good idea too and the truth is he got stung as well, and far worse than we were, because he's ruined now.' No, they'll say: 'That old thief and swindler. He was fleecing us the whole time, I bet he has millions stashed away in some European bank.' That's human nature for you; it's a subject I know something about. Then what will happen? I can see it clearly, and I'm sure you and our friend Kunz can understand it too: they'll be on us like a pack of hounds, they'll sell off everything to try to recuperate at least a cent of every hundred pesos they put into the business. And whichever one of them has least to do, some unemployed relative, or someone recommended a winter break in the country by his doctor, will step off the ferry one fine morning, wave a bunch of papers in our faces, if he takes the trouble, and that will be that. And he will be the person who goes with the vultures into the shed in the afternoon to haggle over prices, take the money, and watch them empty the shelves in two weeks flat. Our fortnightly sales will become one big end of season clearance sale. Just think, if Galvez does hand over the deed, we'll all have to pack up and leave. We're not living like lords, but we do get by. We've all known better times, beyond compare, I agree. I'm not talking for myself, but I can tell just by looking at you. But at least here you have a roof over your head and we eat twice a day. And in your condition. God forbid that your time should come without a house, without this miserable dog kennel, as you so rightly call it. That will be the start of our misfortunes, the most important part, if you like, I don't deny it. But just think too that we're right at the moment when the wheel's about to turn, when Petrus is about to secure the capital he needs to get the shipyard going again. And beyond that, there's help from the government, bonds backed by the nation for the shipyard, the railroad, and all the other things Petrus hasn't even dreamt of yet. I swear to you. At any rate, with the state you're in and while Galvez has got the deed in his pocket, I propose to step up the sales to make sure there's money for you to put aside. The baby is innocent, when all's said and done."

She agreed, but could not have cared less. The ferocity of Galvez's vanished smile seemed to have found refuge in her eyes, in the sweetness of her cheeks, in the pensive eagerness with which she sucked on her cigarette as she stared at the fire, the dogs' heads, or into empty space.

"You don't understand," she said one night, smiling at Larsen with a strange pity. There were just the two of them; she had been trying to fix a wire on the radio, refusing his help. "For example, you can love God or curse him. But God's will is done, and you are left looking on; you get to understand what God's will was from what happens. It's the same with Galvez. From years back, from the start. He might send Petrus to jail; he might burn the certificate. What matters is that I don't know what he's thinking of doing, what he is going to choose. I never wanted to ask him, and still less now, when this is what we've come to, when we're worse off than ever before. By that I don't mean because we're so poor, but because we're trapped. Once he has decided something, I find out, and then I know what's going to happen to me. That's how it is; and I know that's how it must be. The same thing happened with the child. And there's something else you don't understand: you don't understand him. I'm sure he'll never use that certificate to put Petrus in jail. He believed in Petrus, he believed he was his friend, and believed all those tales he told him about getting rich. Petrus lent him money, he paid our tickets here, he took us out to eat, without having to, we'd already decided to come, and he paid not just for Galvez but for me too. When we got here, we also went to stay in the Belgrano, that filthy hole which in those days was a 'modern hotel where many of the top employees of my shipyard reside.' The next day, Galvez went to take up his post, you know, Administrative Manager, the one he's held ever since thanks to his own merits. Listen to this: that morning in the Belgrano he even asked me which tie and shirt he should put on. He had no choice about the suit — he only had two left, so he was forced to wear the lightweight one. He set off, long before starting time, and found that dump, though it wasn't as squalid as it is now, he found that the workforce, the hundreds, thousands or millions of workmen and office employees who 'enjoyed benefits not yet provided for in the most advanced legislation' were rats, bugs, fleas, the odd bat or two, and a gringo called Kunz who had been left behind in a corner where he still sat tracing plans or fiddling with his stamp collection. And when he came back to the Belgrano for lunch, all he said to me was that they were very behind with the accounts and he would have to work a lot outside office hours. I thought then, not that he was mad, but that he wanted to commit suicide, or to start doing so, so slowly that he's still in the process. So I don't think he'll ever take the certificate to the judge. He's not keeping it to get revenge on Petrus, but just so he can think that one day, when he chooses, he could have his revenge, and feel powerful, capable of even more infamy than Petrus himself."

This was at the beginning of Larsen's pursuit of her, for a few days after the evening he had met Diaz Grey, Petrus and Barreiro in Santa Maria, had set foot again in that lost world. Because Galvez continued to spend his evenings far from the cabin, and Larsen's persistent efforts to convince the woman to steal the certificate and give it to him to make everyone happy soon took on an erotic undertone. Larsen sat, elbows on the table, absent-mindedly offering his hand for the dogs to lick, his head protected from the cold by his tilted black hat, every now and then sipping a heavy red wine, and patiently, implacably, retelling his old, successful monologues of seduction (even improving on them, he thought) generous but never final admissions of defeat, sweeping but imprecise offers, the kind of threats which horrify those who make them.

The woman was ever more wrapped in her sullen silence. She did not even look at Galvez when he got up after dinner, put on a loose sailor's jersey over his pullover; made no reply to his gruff goodbye, and did not seem to hear his footsteps as they faded on the frosty mud of the path. She washed the dishes, blinking at the smoke from the cigarette dangling from her mouth, and passed the plates for Larsen to dry.

So beautiful and so done for, Larsen thought. *If only she'd wash and do her hair. But all the same, even if she spent her afternoons in a beauty parlour and had a wardrobe from Paris, and I was ten or twenty years younger, whatever it took, and she was interested in me, even then it would be no use. She's worn smooth, burnt out, parched like a field after a summer fire, deader than my grandmother. It's not impossible that whatever she's carrying inside her is dead as well, I'll wager.*

Then the woman would drag over the demijohn of wine and the two of them would sit hunched at the table, without looking at each other; they drank at their leisure and smoked; the wind whistled round the cabin and pushed its cold fingers in, or the clotted peace of the night allowed them to imagine dogs stretched out towards the still whiteness, the playful throb of boat engines as they slid along the smooth river. They also imagined the distances starting and finishing at the wooden cabin, even when it was windy. But never, Larsen could have sworn, did the woman ever stop to think of the past. She smoked between her coat lapels, her lank, greasy hair silhouetted against the door. She was there, that was all, without a past, with a foetus pushing down on legs she could no longer cross. She said little, seldom responding with anything more than a grimace, a curt nod of the head which robbed all questions of meaning: "I was born and here I am."

But her bitterness, her silence, did not seem to be caused by her poverty, her imminent labour, or the fact that Galvez spent every night at El Chamamé. There were no precise reasons for it. Perhaps she was no longer a person, but merely the vessel for a kind of curiosity, for expectancy. She would hum tangos to herself, and it was not always obvious whether she was listening, whether her smile, or rather the curled corners of her mouth, was related in any way to Larsen's slow, dramatic stories or to her own thoughts about future events. *Just as if an old senseless, stupid habit of abandonment led her to believe anything is possible, that anything can happen right here and now, in the face of reason and a thousand incalculable objections*, Larsen surmised.

But that was not true either, Larsen admitted to himself, at least not completely, not enough to help him define and understand her. So he lifted the glass of wine to his lips to take a good mouthful, at the last moment pushing out his tongue so that all he drank was

was a tiny sip. And then he returned to the charge, in his most imploring, passionate voice, but with an added undertone that suggested he was willing to wait night after night if necessary until she finally understood and gave way.

He no longer mentioned the certificate; he invented subtle allusions to it, talking of the object of his desire as if it were a part of a woman's body that he lusted after, as if he were begging her not only to give him the certificate, but also (and not just symbolically) to give him everything it was in her power to give.

Night after night, always hesitantly at first but more openly as her continued docility became apparent, as she allowed him to believe that her silence, her ear peeking out from under her hair, the faint possibility of a smile, were all part of a confused, latent coquettishness. One of those nights, Larsen was sure that the word certificate — or document, or that piece of paper — uttered by mistake had brought a faint blush to her cheek, the left one that she always turned towards him.

"You want me to steal the piece of paper and give it you. Then everything will be all right, we can carry on selling off the machinery and go on living. But if Galvez had to face losing that document now, he'd feel more alone and lost than if I were to die. Deep down, it's not me he loves but that bit of green paper he clutches to his chest every night before he goes to sleep. I don't mean he really loves it. But for now he needs it more than me. I'm not jealous of a scrap of paper or of his love of revenge."

Beyond them there was El Chamamé, although Larsen never used its existence as a further means of persuasion.

When it was built, it might have been for keeping tools, farm implements and sacks in, for retaining that smell of woodsmoke, henhouse and rancid grease which is far more typical of the countryside than that of trees, fruit or animals. It was one of those small sheds that have a brick wall or two which never seem to have been new, put up by amateur workmen from the remains of another building. The rest of it: beams, tin sheets and planks thrown together with no other idea of architecture than that of the spirit level, no other aid than patience. It stood on its own in the corner of a muddy patch of land, so had obviously never been an addition to a larger dwelling.

El Chamamé was five or six blocks from the shipyard, by the side of the wide track the herds used to climb but which was totally deserted now the abattoir had moved from Puerto Tablada, without a single hoofmark on it, used only by the occasional lonely horserider or a swaying, jolting buggy travelling between the coast and the lonely homesteads. Almost always it was someone who had to take the ferry to Santa Maria for health reasons, for a straightforward illness that was beyond the powers of don Alves, the local quack. Nobody coming to buy or sell, nobody with any money, nobody even with the urge to spend.

In the time of the cattle herdsmen, El Chamamé, nameless and not needing one, consisted of: two lanterns, one over the entrance, which was simply a piece of sacking, and the other hanging from a beam; a bar, made of concave planks supported on trestles; one bottle of rum and two of gin; a talkative old half-breed, a knife handle (and perhaps no more than that) stuck in his belt, who always dressed in shirt and baggy riding trousers and still had a broad whip dangling from his left wrist though it was plain he had not been on a horse in years. In a corner almost beyond the reach of the dim light, a pile of hides.

That was all, and it was enough. When it acquired a name: El Chamamé, with underneath: BIG IMPROVEMENTS DUE TO CHANGE OF OWNER, written on a board nailed crookedly to a stunted plane tree that supposedly separated pavement and road, there was not much to add: a few tables, chairs and bottles, another lantern in the corner where a bandstand had replaced the hides. And on a vertical post, another sign: NO CARRYING OR USE OF ARMS, grandiloquent, unnecessary, put there as a sop to authority, in the guise of a policeman boasting a sergeant's stripes who every night tied his horse up to the little tree.

There was not even any need to get rid of the old man with this knife handle. He did no more than quit the bar for whichever table which would have him. There he was, nimble and full of conversation, but of no more significance than the objects he used to take care of before the renaming: the planks, the lanterns, the bottles. Astute, unflagging, waiting from nightfall to dawn for the right moment (unfailingly spotted) to slip in his "that reminds me of" and launch into another of his well-worn, lying stories. Sharing with the sergeant the right to get drunk without paying — in money at least — and the right to drag along the ground (the sergeant in a cocksure, swaggering way, the old man almost affectionately) the dangling tip of a whip.

There was no need to add anything more, and in fact the only thing which might have been defended as an improvement, apart from the greater choice of speeds the barshelf offered for getting drunk, were the musicians, guitar and accordion, and their natural consequence: the tables pushed back against two walls and the area of watered dust left free for dancing.

There was no need to add anything more because the rest — that is, El Chamamé itself, was provided each night by the customers. They came to make El Chamamé, together each man or woman, a piece of the jigsaw puzzle. Even their accidental absences contributed to it; and they even paid for the privilege.

Where they got the money was always a mystery. Petrus Ltd. had closed down some years earlier, and the farms in the area were too poor to employ permanent labourers. Perhaps some of the men worked on the river, but that could only have accounted for two or three of them: Puerto Astillero was now only a halt, and one of the least busy, on the river journey. The closest factories — the fish canning plants — were a lot further south, between Santa Maria and Enduro. One of the customers was the lad from Belgrano's; another, Machin by name, claimed to own a launch which he hired out in Enduro. All the other men were anonymous, twelve or fifteen of them, a couple of dozen on a Saturday night, their women with unbelievable dresses and make-up, an ill-defined female group, a shifting mass of colours, perfumes and holes in high heels or rope scandals, wearing dancing dresses or pinafores stained with babies' sick and urine.

It was ridiculous to try to fathom where they got the money (one peso for a small glass, two a large one for whatever watered-down brew they ordered) because it was even more impossible for anyone to know where the customers themselves had emerged from, which cave or tree or stone they would scuttle back to as soon as the musicians had refused any more encores and packed away their instruments, until the moment the following night when the old man with the knife butt at his waist climbed unsteadily on to a chair to light the lantern which baldly announced to the world outside the punctual resurrection of El Chamamé.

One Saturday, Larsen went there with Kunz, but got no further than the bar. He examined the women with a kind of horrified fascination, perhaps thinking that any imaginable God would have to exchange his all-purpose fiery hell for small private ones. Each to their own, according to divine justice and their own desserts. Perhaps it even crossed his mind that El Chamamé forever at midnight on a Saturday, endlessly repeated, without musicians who were mortal and stopped playing at dawn to claim their steak and eggs, was the hell that had been set aside for him from the beginning of time, or that he had been earning for himself, depending on how you look at it.

Whatever the reason, he could not bear it. He refused Kunz's offer of a second glass. He refrained from spitting on to the already dusty dance floor (the old man with the knife was struggling with a full watering-can, signalling to the musicians not to repeat the waltz) keeping the thickening saliva in his mouth until they were out in the open so that nobody would see a challenge in what was no more than disgust and a rush of indefinable fear.

But of late Galvez had taken to going there every night. He was friendly with the gaunt, bushy-haired man who had taken the old man's place behind the bar, and who served the tables with precise movements in near silence, chewing on a coca leaf the whole time, his clear, absent gaze full of somnolent hatred as he flitted through the smoke, noise and smells.

Galvez was conservative and moderately cynical in the discussions about the immediate future of the world that he held with the police sergeant, who for his part claimed to have known better places and showed himself to be much more extreme when it came to ways of dealing with decadence and the growing confusion of values. Galvez routinely caressed any woman who had no man with her, or whose man was a friend, and left when the music finished, almost always drunk. On the rare early morning when the sergeant did not invent the excuse of a special secret mission, the two of them made their way back to the shipyard together, rubbing their favourite arguments threadbare, repeating the same old words with fresh energy, the sergeant slumped in the saddle of his walking horse, Galvez hanging on to one of the stirrups.

It was only in El Chamamé that Galvez displayed his broad, gleaming, inexpressive smile, his big teeth bared as if he used them to breathe. Although neither of them realised it, his smile was similar to the look in the bar-owner's eyes as he chewed on his coca leaves ("it keeps me from smoking or drinking") who had confided to him his determination (but not the reason for it) to wring ten thousand pesos, one by one, without regard for how long it took, out of these phantoms, the handful of graveyard denizens who made up El Chamamé's customers.

For some unknown reason, in all the time he was trying unsuccessfully to persuade the woman to steal the forged certificate or to tell him how it could be stolen, Larsen never once mentioned the nights Galvez spent in El Chamamé.

THE SUMMERHOUSE IV
THE CABIN VI

Meanwhile since the day of the scandal, Larsen visited the summerhouse in Petrus' garden every evening: from six to seven in the week, and from five to seven on Saturdays and Sundays.

He did not know whether Petrus was in the house or not, or if he had any knowledge of the summerhouse meetings. In any case, the lofty house, the distant yellow gleam of its lights through the early winter dusk, signified Petrus' presence. And though Larsen occasionally doubted the reality of their meeting in the hotel at Santa Maria, nothing could shake his conviction that he had been entrusted with the mission of recovering the certificate, that there had been a pact between the two of them and a promise of reward. He did not want to ask after Petrus' whereabouts, fearing that the slightest word would draw attention if not to his failure, at least to his tardiness. Also, more obscurely, to find out would have meant to doubt: to doubt Petrus, to doubt even his ability to keep his word. Above all, in the abstract, it would have meant the possibility of doubt itself: and that was the only thing Larsen could not permit himself during those winter days.

The maid Josefina always opened the gate for him promptly. She never responded to the mixture of friendliness and gallantry in his greetings, but ushered him in, alone or with the dog. Each time, and each time more dishearteningly, it was like dreaming an ancient dream. In the end, it was like listening every evening to the narration of the same dream, repeated with the same words, by an unchanging, monotonous, unfeeling voice.

The walk down the long tree-lined avenue, nothing more now than a physical effort during which he was as careful not to think as to avoid stepping in any muddy puddles; the bell, the gate and the moment's wait in the lifeless dusk; the dark, hostile woman; sometimes the dog, always the stupid, brassy barking; the untended garden, the dank, greenish-black cold, the statues' impenetrable whiteness; the slow, painfully slow procession, as if held back by a wall of air, to reach the summerhouse; the woman's nervous laugh in greeting; the lofty yellow lights stretching up to the sky from the upper floor of the house. Then the woman, the wearisome, perpetual mystery, the unavoidable participation in a holy sacrament.

One evening after another. The final inspection of how he looked in the wardrobe mirror of his hotel room at Belgrano's; the summerhouse like a boat to carry him downstream for an hour, two at weekends. All she did was question him and listen; in response to his answers she offered only her laugh and her enthralled air.

She was a woman, undoubtedly a beautiful, haughty woman, and somewhere or other detail by detail, a future was being worked out which would give him, Larsen, the privilege of protecting her and perverting her. But now was a time for waiting, not for hoping.

Creased with cold, using an elbow to stop himself collapsing on to the stone table, almost unconcerned whether or not there was a Petrus sitting up on high in the house revelling in his glory, bathed in the coppery light and the supposed comfort of the warm air, Larsen deliberately put on a gruff voice and spoke. At first he would narrate in an orderly fashion, respecting the obvious rules of logic and communication. He began with his friends, when he was eighteen, some women, a dreary portrait with street corner, pool hall, honeysuckle, a few family touches artfully thrown in.

And since she was no one, since she could only respond with a snort and her half-open mouth flecked with saliva, Larsen soon forgot his audience and began to tell himself, evening after evening, the memories still capable of interesting him. He delivered a fierce recital of undoubted episodes that had remained fresh in his mind because even now it was impossible for him fully to understand them, even now he was unable to work out how he had become mixed up in them.

So in the evening's icy gloom, with no other listener but this intermittent hoarse, hysterical laugh, but the hint of a pair of breasts like moons, he told his story without any other purpose than to gain time. With a few alterations dictated by his sense of shame or by vanity, he was able to talk and to lie about everything; she did not take in a word.

Then, almost at once, it was 22 August, a day without promise or threat which managed to keep its secret until the very last moment. The day dawned cloudy, but before noon the sky was as clear and still as all the ones before. The moon rose late and full, shining coldly, windless and harsh, on the water, the shipyard and the winter crops.

A day like any other, although afterwards Larsen was to recall premonitions he had never grasped, unmistakable signs paraded before him which he failed to recognise.

He left the General Manager's office at six, went to Belgrano's for his afternoon shave, arrived at Petrus' gate punctually at seven. Angelica Ines had been dreaming of horses, or invented a dream with horses. Larsen had begun to take her dreams, the brief accounts she gave of them in sudden bursts in her feeble, awed voice as challenges, as set themes. Confident of the wealth of his memory, concerned only to choose the right story, he listened with a patient smile to the confused indications she offered him.

On this occasion it was "that horse licking me to wake me up and warn me of danger before it died." He waited for silence, then began to talk of his love for horses and many other things which had existed in the dead world of the past. For the first time, he felt it was beyond him. This was a love story, and he had to give up the role of hero. More than anything else, he wanted to dissolve into the darkness of the summerhouse and conjure into life, though neither for him nor for her, a sunny afternoon that brought together minutes from many others. He spoke of his disinterested love for a horse which had many coats and names, an animal that only treachery could defeat, he spoke of its legs, of an encounter, its head, its courage on one single occasion and forever afterwards, the pride and joy of a lost breed. It is always hard to talk of love, and impossible to explain it; even more so if the one who hears or reads about it has never experienced it, and more so still if all that is left to the storyteller is the memory of the simple facts which gave birth to his love.

One afternoon of winter sun, a track, a crowd, a three minute frenzy. Perhaps he had been able to see something; the horses seeming to be running for all eternity, with no apparent effort, tiny and remote; the crowd turning from prophecy to urgent demand; his friends hoarse with shouting, the proof of loyalty in the bundle of tickets in his pocket now worth exactly what he had paid for them. Larsen had no idea whether she could make all this out, understand it: he couldn't bring himself to translate some of the terms: grandstand, place bet, final straight, boxed in, odds, stewards' enquiry. But he did realise that all he had done was to make a roundabout confession of his love for a horse or two or three horses, his love of life, his love of the memory of having loved life. It was eight o'clock by the time he finished. He leaned over at the summerhouse doorway to give and receive a pursed, dry kiss.

He became aware once more of winter and old age, of the need to seek respite in harshness and madness. He made his way back to the shipyard, stepping carefully round the muddy dips in the waste ground, guided finally by the yellow gleam from the cabin. He climbed the three planks and went into the warmth without seeing the woman. The dogs came up to sniff the cold on him. He kicked them out of the way, aiming for their snouts, then went and looked closely at the calendar on the wall. Without caring he learnt that sunset had been at 18.26 pm, that there was a full moon, and that he and the rest of the world were rejoicing in the day of the Immaculate Heart of Mary.

The woman came in from the weather, her feet silent on the boards until she got to the centre of the room. He turned to look at her, take his hat off. Perhaps the name of Mary, which he was just beginning to fully understand, altered everything; perhaps the transformation came from the woman's face, her eyes and her smile beneath the spiky, dusty crown of her stiff hair.

"Good evening señora," Larsen said, with a brief nod. He felt fear like an added cold, like a new way of feeling the sensation of cold. "I was over this way and decided to call in. To see how things were. I can go to Belgrano's and get something to eat. Or better still, I'd be very pleased if you would come out to the restaurant with me. I'll bring you back, of course. And in case Galvez shows up, we can leave him a note, a couple of lines. You must have seen the moon: it's like daylight. We can walk slowly so you won't get tired. Cover your head against the dew."

The woman had not closed the door, and above her messy hair, above her eyes and her smile, Larsen was talking politely to the white moonlight, gaining minutes that were useless to him.

It was not the kind of fear he could explain honestly to a long-lost friend, to someone crushed but recognisable who had surfaced from death or oblivion. *The moment comes when some unimportant, meaningless event forces us to wake up, to look at things as they really are.* It was a fear that it was all a farce, a fear of the first real warning that the game was being played independently of him,

141

of Petrus, of all those who had been sure they were playing by choice, sure that all they had to do was say no, for the game to come to an end.

The woman was leaning back against the table, her body exhausted, her head held high. The dogs were at her side, jumping up half-heartedly every now and then at the overcoat drawn tight over her belly.

Larsen could see himself, diminished and in mourning, re-treating to the wooden wall and the black number on the calendar, clutching his hat, a kindly, distracted look on his face. He was thinking that the only possible consolation lay in surrender and ridicule.

"What a night. So cold: tomorrow everything will be white with frost. But we can't say we weren't warned it would be a full moon."

He sighed and shook his head. As he took out his handkerchief to mop his forehead, his wrist brushed against the revolver under his arm.

"A full moon."

The dogs were stretched out, only occasionally lifting their heads expectantly towards the woman's body. Larsen turned to look at her again: she was exactly as she had been when she came in, showing no sign of having heard or seen him. The same fixed, empty smile, painful but bearable because the eyes had lost all capacity for mockery, accusation or curiosity. Or they were only looking with a twin, impersonal curiosity: she was no longer a person, but the act, the faculty of seeing; and what was seen, Larsen, the room, the yellow light, the faint vapour of their breaths, were simply points of reference, confirmation of a certainty.

"It's starting," Larsen was thinking. He leaned forward and said, with an almost forlorn smile: "It's starting."

She nodded, raised a hand for him to wait. The table creaked as she bent forward. She jerked her head to one side, away from him.

Snatches of distant music reached them. A stuttering, intrusive motor engine was coming down the cattle drive. She turned slowly, not so fearful now, towards him, her face screwed up like a child's, the eyes shrunken with tears.

"Promise you won't leave me alone tonight, and I'll tell you what you want to know. Promise me you won't go until I ask you to."

"I promise," Larsen said, holding up two fingers.

She hesitated, looking at him discouraged. "All right. If I asked, it was because I wanted to believe you."

She shuffled over to a bench and sat down. Standing beside the calendar, Larsen could see her in profile, beaded with sweat despite the chill, appearing to listen but frightened to hear, as if absorbed in the taste of the lip she was sucking. She was ugly, unkempt and sallow-looking, but Larsen felt she was more fearsome than ever, secret, untouchable.

"Whatever is eating her tonight, whatever it is, her belly or her jealousy or what the moonlight suddenly showed her — it's doing it with her permission, with her approval. While it eats her, it feeds her. Perhaps the moonlight outside reminded her she is a human being, and even more to my advantage, a woman. She realised she's living in this doghouse, and not even alone, but seen and frustrated by a man, a stranger, anyone, because he no longer loves her. No, it's the other way round, she is a woman even if she doesn't look like it; a man who is a stranger because she doesn't love him any longer. Maybe she went outside to do something and looked back here by mistake, seeing the planks and boards, the three chained steps. Everything looked new and strange in the moonlight. She was forced to measure her misery, her years, all the time wasted, the little she has left to misspend."

"When I tell you to go," the woman said, "you leave, and don't say a word to anyone. If you meet Galvez, don't tell him you were with me."

She wiped her face on her sleeve, then looked up at him,

suddenly serene. The glinting sweat made her look younger. Her eyes and smile spoke of nothing beyond an offer of connivance.

"Not yet," she murmured. "Now I know for sure. But it doesn't matter, I'll keep my promise. There must be some cognac left. Galvez always arrives home drunk, he never drinks here. Out of respect for me. Respect…" The second time she said the word, she paused on each syllable, as though pondering on its meaning. Then she guffawed, looked out into the night: "You'd better shut the door. Give me a cigarette. The certificate isn't here anymore, and I don't think Galvez has it either. The truth is I was going to steal it for you, but all of a sudden he went crazy and began to love that bit of paper as if it were another person. I could see it was the only thing in the world he cared for. A green piece of paper. I'm sure he couldn't have lived without it."

Larsen lit her a cigarette, then traced a maze of steps to the door and back to fetch the already opened bottle from under the bed. He found a tin mug and brought it to the table; pulled up a crate and eased his body down until he was sitting on it. He dropped his hat on his knees and lit himself a cigarette. He had no desire to smoke it, but watched as it burnt down between his fingers, glinting off his clean, oiled nails. He would not look at the woman.

"You don't drink, do you?" He poured himself a slug of brandy and looked thoughtful. "So the certificate isn't here. And Galvez doesn't have it either. What about Kunz?"

"What would the German care about it?" She was still crouched over, but her face was calm and even amused. "It happened this afternoon. There was nothing I could do about it, even if I had wanted to. At about three o'clock, Galvez came back from the yard. He sat here for a while, glancing at me furtively, saying nothing. When I asked if he needed anything, he shook his head. He was sitting on the bed over there. I was scared because it was the first time in a long while I had seen him look happy. He was looking at me like a young man. I got fed up of asking him, so I went out to do the washing. I was hanging it out when he came up behind me and caressed my face. He had shaved and was wearing a clean shirt he hadn't asked me for. "Everything is going to be all right," he said; but I knew he was only thinking of himself. "How?" I asked him. All he did was laugh and stroke me; it really seemed as though everything was all right for him. I was pleased he was so happy, I didn't ask him any more questions, but let him caress me and kiss me for as long as he liked. Perhaps he was saying goodbye, but I didn't ask him that either. Soon afterwards he left, not going towards the yard but down behind the back of the sheds. I stared after him, he seemed so much younger, he was walking so quickly and determinedly. Just as he was on the point of disappearing, he stopped and came back. I stood there waiting, but as he came nearer I realised he hadn't changed his mind. He told me he was going to Santa Maria to hand over the certificate to the court, I think he said, and to press charges. He said it as if it were very important to me, as if he were doing it for me, as if those were the nicest words he could say to me, and I was longing to hear them. Then he left for real. I went on hanging out the wash, this time without staring after him."

Larsen chose to pretend he was angry, pretend he was interested.

"Strange I didn't see him or hear anything of him. He can't have caught the ferry in Puerto Astillero. If he was here at three and stayed a while, he can't have reached Santa Maria in time to get to the court. That shuts at five. And it's an hour's journey . . ."

"After I'd finished with the washing I could feel twinges, so I came in to rest on the bed. But I had forgotten the pain before it eased, because something suddenly occurred to me, as if someone had said it aloud. I jumped off the bed and rummaged through the wardrobe. There aren't many clothes in it, only clippings from the papers that he kept because they mentioned the shipyard and the lawsuit. I found the jar of molasses we used to hide money in for when my time comes. It's got a narrow top, so it was hard to get the money out. We thought that after the child was born, one of us would smash it open. I stuck a knitting needle in it. Galvez had done the same before leaving. I haven't the faintest idea how much we had saved. That was when I realised he was gone for good. I didn't want to cry; I wasn't mad or sad, just stunned. I already told you that as he walked off he seemed much younger. I began to think he looked even younger than the day I met him. A Galvez just out of the army, before he met me, walking away through the nettles, shaking off the dust. He won't be back, he's another person, he has nothing more to do with me or with you. What will you do now? You can't do a thing, you have to wait until I give you permission to leave."

She smiled, as if her refusal to let him go and all the other things she had said were merely a joke, nothing but banter she had made up on the spur of the moment to keep him there and to flirt with him.

"So that's how things are," Larsen said. "Well, I have to tell you that what Galvez has done means the end for all of us. And he goes and does it just when everything was about to be sorted out. It's a real shame."

But she was not listening. She sat on the bench deaf to his words, staring disdainfully at the square patch of white night in the miserable window.

Perhaps he hasn't gone to Santa Maria. If he took the money he may be drunk in El Chamamé. I'll go and talk to him. Not even now could Larsen feel indignation or interest. So the two of them sat there silent and still, Larsen taking sips from the tin mug and sneaking glances at the woman; the woman now with a mocking, astonished look on her face, as if recalling the absurdity of a recent dream. They sat like that for a long while, the cold seeping into them, infinitely far apart. She shivered; her teeth began to chatter.

"You can go now," she said, staring at the window. "I'm not throwing you out; but there's no point in your staying."

Larsen waited for her to stand up. Then he got up and placed his hat on the table. As he came forward, he saw the mound of the overcoat, the straining buttonholes, the safety pin closing the neck. He had no desire to do it; he could think of nothing which might take the place of desire. He stared at her sallow, shiny face, the impassive eyes which had already judged him. He gently pressed his stomach against hers, then kissed her, scarcely holding her shoulders, the palms of his hands rubbing against the rough cloth. She let him do it, opened her mouth; she stood still, breathing hard, for as long as Larsen wished. Then she stepped back until she bumped into the table and slowly, deliberately, lifted her hand and slapped Larsen across the cheek and ear. The slap made him happier than the kiss, more believing in hope and salvation.

"Señora," he murmured. They stood there eyeing each other wearily, with a faint content, a tiny warm glow of hatred, as if they really were a man and a woman.

"Go now," she said. She had tucked both hands back in her overcoat pockets. She was calm, sleepy, the corners of her mouth edged with shy satisfaction.

Larsen picked up his hat and walked to the door as quietly as he could.

"You and I . . ." she began.

Larsen heard her laugh softly, listening to the guttural, lazy sound. He waited for her to be silent, then turned round, not so much to look at her as to show the nostalgia on his own face, a grimace calling for respect more than understanding.

"For us too there was a time when we might have met," he said. "And always of course, as you said, a time before that."

"Go," the woman repeated.

Before he went down the three steps, before the moonlight and a more bearable solitude, Larsen muttered a kind of excuse to himself: "It happens to everyone."

The Shipyard VI

Larsen was unable to find Galvez that night or the ones following. It was verified that he had not filed any charges at the Santa Maria courthouse. He did not reappear at the cabin or the yard. In the dank general office, Larsen's only companion was a monosyllabic, listless Kunz, who constantly drank maté tea as he shuffled ancient blueprints for ships and machinery that had never been built, or shifted the stamps around in his album.

Kunz no longer came into the General Manager's office, and Larsen could raise no enthusiasm for what was in the files. Like someone very sick, he knew the end was near. He could recognise all the external symptoms, but relied even more on the signals of utter boredom and apathy conveyed by his own body.

Without fully knowing why, and caring even less, he sceptically took advantage of the scant morning energy to while away a few hours with stories of salvage, repairs, debts, legal battles. The cold grey light through the window sparked his determination to stay hunched over these long-dead matters. His lips formed the syllables; he listened to the soft sound at the corners of his mouth.

That took up the couple of hours until noon. He could still slap Kunz on the back and walk down the iron staircase behind him, keeping up the pretence, erect, broad-shouldered, a thoughtful expression on a face that admitted no defeat.

Kunz did the lunch-time cooking now. One morning, without warning, without consulting the woman, he had made the fire and taken the vegetables she was washing from her. The three of them talked of the weather, of the dogs, of any rare items of news, of how the winter was affecting fishing or the crops.

But in the afternoon, Larsen found it impossible to bend over the files and pronounce the long-lost names in silence. It was then that his solitude and failure became solid presences in the freezing air, and he lapsed into a state of torpor. He had lost all hope that his hatred of Galvez could offer him interest or salvation, that the opportunity for vengence, the need to perform all the steps necessary for revenge, could give a sense of purpose to his existence.

Those afternoons, the overcast or forlornly clear skies gazed in through the broken window, enfolding an old man who had given up on himself, who did nothing to protest while his head was taken over by a jumble of memories, fragments of ideas, images that sprang from no inner source. From two till six, the biting air caught at the unhealthy, drooping face of an old man, the bottom lip of his slack mouth juddering as he drew breath. The grey light touched on the round, near-bald cranium, darkening the single tuft of hair scraped across the forehead. It accented the thin, curved nose, that still stood out proudly from the decaying, greasy face. As if keeping time, the bloodless mouth drooped down the cheeks, then suddenly twitched up again. A baffled old man, starting to drool, one thumb hooked in his waistcoat, his body swaying to and fro between chair and desk as if he were riding the bumps in a cart carrying him off down rutted country roads.

And as everything must come about, there were those who saw how the boats from the north and the islands were beginning to unload the tiny suns of oranges; others noticed how the noonday sun was starting to warm the water in the drinking troughs, and brought out dogs, cats and tiny, vacillating flies. Still others noted that a few trees were persisting in sending forth buds even though they were scorched by the night-time frost. It may be that the letter was in some way connected to all these mysteries.

It happened one Thursday. At lunch-time, the ferry brought a letter, and Poetters, the owner of the Belgrano, sent the boy round to the yard with it. He pressed the bell for a while with no success, then clambered up to the general office, where Kunz was carefully copying a faded plan on to a squared-off sheet of vellum. It was a ten-year-old design for a perforator capable of punching a hundred holes a minute. Kunz knew that in the distant world beyond, they were selling machines that could drill five hundred holes a minute. He was spending seven hours a day on this plan because he thought he could improve the old design, which he had found while he was cleaning out a blocked drain. He was sure that, with a few modifications, the perforator could, in theory at least, be made to drill a hundred and fifty holes every sixty seconds.

He gave the boy a hostile reception. The sight of the envelope disturbed him.

"It's for señor Larsen," the boy pointed out.

"I can see that," Kunz retorted. "If it's a tip you're after, better come back at Christmas. If it's something else, I'm not the one to give it you."

The boy muttered a mild insult in his high-pitched voice and left. Kunz stood motionless in the centre of the vast office, slowly recovering from his astonishment and doubt, staring respectfully, superstitiously, remorsefully, at the commonplace typed envelope, the wine-coloured stamp stuck on askew. TO THE GENERAL MANAGER OF PETRUS LTD., PUERTO ASTILLERO.

Dumbfounded, unable to bring himself to believe, considering himself unworthy of such belief, he peered closely at the letter. In the early days after Petrus had given him permission to call himself the Technical Manager, the odd letter, circular or catalogue still arrived from forgetful manufacturers or machinery importers, together with others from banks or income tax offices which were sent on to the Creditors Committee in the capital. After a few months, these last scraps of proof that the shipyard existed in the real world, for someone apart from the phantom managers it still sheltered, trailed off altogether. So Kunz gradually lost his faith, swept up in the universal scepticism. The huge derelict building became the abandoned temple of an extinct religion. Nor could the prophecies of resurrection which old man Petrus recited from time to time, distributed to all and sundry by Larsen, return him to a state of grace.

But now all these years later, he was holding in his hand a letter addressed to the shipyard by the world outside, like some irrefutable proof which triumphantly clinches a theological debate. A miracle announcing the presence and truth of a God whom he, Kunz, had blasphemed.

Anxious to kindle the faith in another soul, and to warm himself at its fire, he rushed into the General Manager's office without knocking. He saw the old, stupefied man rocking behind the desk, hands dangling useless above the jumble of files; eyes bulging, empty of questions. But Kunz took none of this in. He put the envelope on the desk within Larsen's reach and merely said, confident that he was saying it all:

"Look. A letter."

Larsen emerged from nothingness into a loneliness that was impervious to anything that man or events could fashion. Then slowly he smiled, and began to scrutinise the envelope. He started by doing something Kunz had overlooked: he examined the postmark, reading the semicircle that spelt out Santa Maria. As he carefully slit the envelope open, he vaguely thought of Petrus. The soul of discretion, Kunz had edged over to the window to fill his pipe. He turned round sharply at the first curse. Larsen was on his feet, alive again, holding the letter out to him. Kunz read falteringly, suddenly ashamed at himself for ever having believed.

To: The General Manager of Jeremias Petrus Limited.
Dear Sir:
I am making so bold as to divert your attention from your duties
to tender you my resignation as Administrative Manager, a post
I have occupied in the firm for more years than I care to recall,
to the general approval of all responsible citizens of our country.
I waive any claim to the back pay owing to me which I neglected
to collect at the time. I further renounce any claim to the equal
third of the proceedings from all the thefts which you have
ordered from the sheds. I should add that this morning as soon
as he stepped from the ferry Jeremias Petrus was placed under
arrest, as a consequence of the report I made to the authorities a
few days ago concerning the forged documents about which I
had previously taken the trouble to inform you. I was at the
quayside with the police officer, but señor Petrus pretended not
to see me. I suppose he could not bring himself to admit the
existence of such blackhearted ingratitude. I gather in Santa
Maria that you are not welcome in the city. That is unfortunate,
since I was hoping you might come to see me to convince me I
had made a mistake, and to outline in detail for me the glorious
future you and I are to enjoy, tomorrow or the next day. It
would have been amusing.

Yours etc.

A. GALVEZ

"The cunning son of a bitch," muttered Larsen with thoughtful
astonishment.

Kunz let the letter fall, then stooped to pick up the envelope and
stamp that Larsen had thrown on to the floor. He walked slowly
back to his own office, to the blue sheet of vellum he had been
drawing on.

Larsen knew at once what he must do. He might have known it even before the letter arrived or at least, he had within him the seeds of the actions he could foresee, and which he was condemned to carry out. As if it were true that every human act is born before it is committed, exists prior to its encounter with a random agent. Larsen knew what he needed, inescapably, to do. But he had no interest in finding out why. He also knew that it was as dangerous to do what was required, as to refuse to do so. Once he had glimpsed what was to be done, to refuse would mean that the act, denied the space and life it craved, would grow inside him, bitter and monstrous, until it devoured him from within. To agree to carry it out — and he had not only accepted, but had begun to accomplish it — meant that the act would feed voraciously on the last of his strength.

He was accustomed to finding support in farce. He was so desperate he had no need of any witness. With a defiant, pitying smile, he took off his coat and jacket, glanced down at the white linen bulge of his shoulder holster over the grubby shirt. He put the revolver on his desk and ejected the bullets.

He sat there apparently engrossed in his thoughts, pressing the trigger over and over again until the calm late winter afternoon began to draw to a close, crouching in the centre of a harsh silence barely impinged on by dogs, cattle, the horns of distant boats tossing on the river.

At six, perished with cold, he put the bullets back in the drum and the revolver back in its holster. He donned his hat and overcoat, then pressed the buzzer to call in the Technical Manager. Kunz came to the door with the slightly weary but contented expression of a man who has performed his daily duty. He watched him come and go between the window and the telephone switchboard, head sunk on chin, hands behind his back, one shoulder twisted forward, the tuft of hair scraped over his brow. Kunz's scant respect for Larsen had diminished still further since his recent loss of faith. Lighting his crackling pipe, he settled to wait in silence, anticipating his disbelief. Larsen's head appeared at Kunz's shoulder and slowly straightened up. To Kunz it seemed more alive, harsher; the gleam in the eyes and the senile cruelty of the mouth put him on his guard.

"Those buyers," Larsen said. "We've got to phone them straightaway and tell them we want to sell. And we've got to let them understand we won't haggle over prices. But they have to come today, whatever the time. Understand? I'll deal with them."

"I can give them a call. But I doubt they'll come today. Perhaps first thing tomorrow . . ."

"Call them. And I want you please to be here. We're going to sell a few things. Only what's needed to get to Santa Maria and to find that son of a bitch. Or to hire lawyers for Petrus. I don't know whether I should ask you to come with me; we may need someone to stay here at the yard."

Kunz shook his head. He was at peace, not interested in men or gods; his only link with the world was his imaginary perforator.

"What good will it do you if you find Galvez?" he asked. "So you insult him, fight him, kill him. Petrus will still be in jail, and they'll send someone to throw us out of here."

"That might have worried me before. But when that letter arrived, or from the moment it was written, everything changed. All this is finished, or as good as; all we can do now is choose if it ends one way or another."

"Whatever you say," Kunz replied. "I'll phone the scrap merchants."

So that night, after sending the boy from Belgrano's with a message to Petrus' house, after looking at himself in the deceitful mirror of his room first as at a stranger, then as at the unmoving face of a dead friend, lastly as at a mere human probability, Larsen walked, tall and courteous, between the two buyers to the shed door lit by their distant headlamps. Kunz preceded them with two lanterns. He hung them up, then stood outside the door, unwilling to have anything to do with the business.

Slumped on a packing case, hands thrust in his coat pockets, Larsen made as if to direct the operation, silently fuming but determined not to discuss the two men's offers. They roamed all over the shed, occasionally taking one of the lanterns with them to inspect a dark, frozen corner. Then they dragged some object or other back to the pool of light that shone from the other lantern above Larsen's head. They stepped back, immediately repenting in tandem at their choice. Larsen agreed with a ferocious:

"You're right, friend. It's rotten, all rusted up, it'll never work. It would be daylight robbery to make you pay anything for it. How much?"

He listened to their offer, accepted with a nod of the head, then uttered a single curse, meant in the plural. When he had sold enough for the thousand pesos he reckoned he needed, he stood up and passed round cigarettes.

"I'm sorry, but that's it. Hand over the cash and load up. There's no receipt and we don't take cheques."

Kunz came in to fetch the lanterns, then walked away across the waste lot, leaning into the rising south wind, a globe of white light in each hand. Still quaking with anger as he stood by the departing truck, Larsen saw Kunz put out the lanterns under the eaves of the cabin.

SANTA MARIA V

So began Larsen's last trip down-river to the cursed city. He probably realised on the way that he had come to say goodbye, that his pursuit of Galvez was no more than the necessary pretext, the excuse. Those of us who saw and recognised him then found him even older, beaten, desolate. But there was something different about him too, though it was something forgotten from before rather than anything new: a harshness, an arrogance, a mood that recalled an earlier Larsen, the one who had arrived in Santa Maria five or six years before filled with hope and his obsession.

He was showing us — the few who were able to see it — a rough and ready, patched up version of the Larsen he had been before the shipyard had so altered him. His body, his clothes were that much more worn, the lock of hair across his forehead that much sparser, the twitches of mouth and shoulder that much more frequent. But — we feel sure of it now — it was in no way hard for us to imagine his former self's movements, his gait, the provocation and casual assurance of his stares and smiles. That is what all those of us in a position to compare must have sensed when he crossed the new square at midday or dusk, his heels patiently scoring the gravel; when he climbed on to a bar-stool in the Plaza and drank calmly and openly, though with a subtle scorn that his expression and his words belied; when he politely stopped someone in the street to ask a tourist's question about changes and progress in the city; when he leaned casually against the bar of the Berna, accepting without demur that the owner pretended not to remember him, looking us over without curiosity, secure in his absolute certainty — all that must have told us that Larsen had wiped us from his mind, that he was succeeding in making his farewell as easy and painless as possible by retreating five years into the past. He was occupying a position from which it was impossible for him to know who we were, or what we meant to him; to know what was going on, in fact.

They saw him, we saw him do the rounds of all the town's cafés, canteens and liquor stores for two nights; saw him stubbornly comb the shacks of the coast filled with guitar music and drinking, talking readily and with no apparent hurry, offering drinks generously, showing a hitherto unsuspected acceptance of the world. We heard him ask for Galvez, for a smiling, balding but still young man who it would be hard to mistake for anyone else, or to forget. But none of us had seen him, or no one was sure, or wanted to lead Larsen to him.

So that Larsen, by all accounts, abandoned the main reason for his trip: revenge, and devoted the third day to a no less absurd or insincere objective: a visit to Petrus.

On that afternoon, the Santa Maria jail, which all of us residents over thirty still called "The Outpost", was a new, white building. At the front gate stood a glass-walled sentry box with a cement roof which even today boasts its immensely tall flagpole. Though little more than a glorified police station, it now fills a quarter of a block on the north side of the Old Square. On the afternoon in question it was still a one storey building, although bags of cement, staircases and scaffolding were being collected to start work on the second.

Visits to prisoners were between three and four. Larsen sat on a bench at the edge of the circular square. It was full of dark, damp green colours, with worn moss-covered paving stones, and was surrounded by old colonial houses painted pink and cream, hermetic behind their ironwork, dark patches staining their façades at every threat of rain. He stared at the green-stained bronze statue and its astoundingly laconic inscription: BRAUSEN: FOUNDER. As he smoked a cigarette in the sun it occurred to him that in every city, in every house, in himself even, there existed a quiet perimeter, a spot where people could seek refuge as they struggled to survive the events life imposed on them. An exclusion zone, a place of blindness, of small, slow insects, of redoubts, of sudden, never properly understood, never well-timed, moments of reversal.

It was precisely three o'clock when he acknowledged the blue uniform behind the sentrybox glass. He turned at the door to the outpost to look back at the bronze man on his horse, unconvincing, stolid in the bleached winter sunlight.

(When the monument was unveiled, we discussed for months in the Plaza, in the club, in more humdrum public meeting places, at conversations over dinner and in the columns of *El Liberal*, the accoutrements the artist had bestowed on the "quasi-eponymous" hero, as the governor called him in his speech. This phrase must have required a lot of thought: it did not openly suggest the renaming of Santa Maria, but it hinted that the provincial authorities might go along with any campaign launched with that in mind. There were arguments over: the poncho, seen as too Northern; the boots, as too Spanish; the jacket, as too military; the hero's profile was criticised as being too semitic; his features were said to be too cruel, sardonic, and the eyes too close-set; some said his body was so tilted it looked as though he was a novice on horseback; others that the horse was wrong because it was Arab and ungelded. Last but not least, the siting of the statue was criticised for being anti-historical and absurd as it committed the Founder to be eternally galloping back south, as if he had regretted it all and was scurrying back to the distant plains he had abandoned when he came to give us a name and a future.)

Hat in hand, Larsen made his way along the cold, tiled corridor and came to a halt at the desk, the uniform, the half-breed with his drooping moustache.

"Afternoon . . ." he smiled with a disdain, a scorn that forty years had tempered. He handed over his identity papers unopened. "I've come to see señor Petrus, don Jeremias Petrus, if that is all right with you."

Then he walked along an echoing emptiness, turned left and stood waiting while another man in uniform, this time standing with a Mauser on his hip, asked him some questions. An old man in cardigan and slippers went and came, jerked his head at Larsen to follow him, then led the way down another labyrinth of straight lines, colder still, impregnated with the smell of disinfectant and cellar. The old man stopped by a fire extinguisher, pushed open an unlocked door.

"How long can I stay?" Larsen asked, peering into the gloom.

"Until you get bored," the old man replied with a shrug. "We'll settle up later."

Larsen went in and stood still until he heard the sound of the door closing. He was not in a cell; the room was an office piled with furniture, stepladders and pots of paint. He went forward with a smile of greeting on his face, but found he was heading the wrong way, stumbling through a strong smell of turpentine. Suddenly to his right he discovered the prisoner sitting in a corner behind a big, rectangular desk. He was tiny, freshly shaven, alert, as if he had been lying in wait for him, as if he had planned the arrangement of the furniture just to catch him off guard, as if this initial advantage might guarantee him the upper hand in their talk.

He looked older and even more bony; his sidewhiskers were longer and whiter, his glittering eyes even more disturbing. His hands were resting on the leather back of a closed briefcase which was the only thing on the desk's green baize rectangle. At almost his first glance, Larsen regained the enthusiasm, the vague sense of envy which had crumbled during his absence from Petrus.

"Well, here we are," he said.

Petrus, excited but in control, flashed the tip of a tooth, then snapped his mouth shut again. It went back to being merely a thin, sinuous, horizontal line. Perhaps for it to become like that Petrus had not needed to repeat scorn and refusals from childhood — perhaps over the centuries others had done it for him, and bequeathed him this mouth that was no more than a minimal slit for eating and talking. *A mouth that could cease to exist without anyone noticing. A mouth which protects him from the disgust of intimacy and delivers him from temptation. A pit, a barrier.* A soft grey light filtered into the room through a curtain which obscured most of the balcony; at one end a long narrow triangle of August sun spilled in softly. A black leather sofa stood against the curtain, covered with neatly folded rugs. On top rested a small, flat, hard pillow. That must be Petrus' bedroom corner, so different to the one in his house on pillars by the riverside, where the pillows were plump and covered with embroidery bearing significant family dates, rustic decorations, or the unsuspected double meaning of the saying: *Ein gutes Gewissen ist ein sanftes Ruhekissen.*

"Here we are," Petrus repeated sourly. "But not as we were before. Take a seat. I don't have much time, there are lots of problems I still have to look into."

"Just a moment, please," Larsen said. He was prepared to be respectful, but not servile. He left his hat on the edge of the green desk top, went over to the curtain and lifted a corner with exactly the same curious, unthinking gesture that, years later, Inspector Carner would make morning and night in his office on the floor above.

Larsen could see the horse's stained croup, and the S-shape sketched by its tail, but the branches of the plane trees prevented him from making out anything more than the fringe of the

Founder's poncho and a high boot casually thrust into its stirrup. Steadfastly, Larsen strove to understand that moment in his life and in the world: the dark, twisted trees with their fresh leaves; the light glinting off the horse's bronze haunches; the stillness, the patient secrecy of a provincial afternoon. He let the curtain drop, defeated but without resentment; he turned back into the room to face other truths, other lies swaying back and forth to help his memory, he took a chair and sat down, a moment before Petrus' cold, patient voice called out:

"Please, take a seat won't you?"

Why this and not something else, anything else. It's all the same. Why him and me, and not two other men?

He's in jail, finished; every crease of his white and yellow skull is telling me there are no more excuses for deceiving myself, for living, for any kind of passion or bravado.

"I've been expecting you for days. I could not believe you would desert me. Nothing has changed as far as I am concerned; I might even say, without being indiscreet, that things have noticeably improved since our last encounter. In fact, I am temporarily out of reach, taking a breather. This absurd notion of locking me up for a while is my enemy's last ploy, the worst they can hit me with. A few days longer in this office — a little less comfortable than others maybe, but essentially the same — and our run of bad luck will be over. I'm not wasting any time. They've been so kind as to prevent anyone making me waste time so that I can concentrate on sorting out my problems at leisure, once and for all. I know I can tell you: I've found a solution to all the difficulties that were holding back the forward march of the company."

"I'm glad to hear it," Larsen said. "Everyone will be thrilled when I go back to the yard and tell them. If you give me permission to do so, that is."

"Yes, you can, but only tell the senior staff, the ones who have demonstrated their loyalty. I have not bothered to find out why I am being detained here. But it seems it's something to do with that famous certificate we talked of. What happened? Did you fail in the mission I entrusted you with, or did you go over to my enemies?"

Larsen smiled, took his time to get out a cigarette and light it. Then he forced himself to cast a baleful glance at the fanatic, expectant gull's head peering at him, a head assured of every victory, confident that no one could prevent it being right to the very end.

"You know I didn't," Larsen said slowly. "That's why I'm here. That's why I came as soon as I heard you'd been arrested."

He would have liked to say: *I did all I could. I put up with humiliations, and inflicted some. I used violence of a kind you know as well as I do, exactly as well as I do, and which cannot be described by the victim in a charge sheet because he cannot understand it, cannot separate it from his suffering and realise that it is its cause. You must have used violence like that every single day. I bet you know all the rest too, you are the same as me, no better, both of us are men and we know the opportunities for infamy are commonplace and finite: cunning, loyalty, tolerance, sacrifice even, clutching on to someone as if you were saving him from a rushing river, helping instead to drown him, almost always at his request, exactly when it suits us.*

"The only thing I did wrong was to fail," Larsen said.

Petrus pulled in his head like a tortoise. His yellowing teeth glinted once again, this time more openly. He did not condemn Larsen entirely; his sunken, gleaming eyes sought him out with a mixture almost of pity and amused curiosity.

"All right, I trust you. I've always been a good judge of men," Petrus said after a pause. "It doesn't matter, in fact. I can prove I was unaware of the existence of any forged documents. At least, no one can prove I knew anything. Let's forget it. What is important is that justice will soon be done: in days, a couple of weeks at the most. Now more than ever we need a capable, trustworthy man in charge of the shipyard. Do you have the strength and the faith to be that man?"

Larsen tried to buy time with a vigorous nodding of his head. He was struggling to get his lungs used to the rarified air of banishment which now all at once seemed to him unbearable, palpable, even though he had been breathing it all winter long. An air which at first was barely tolerable, but which eventually became almost impossible to do without.

"You can count on me," he said, and the old man smiled. "But the truth is I've wasted a lot of time at the yard, and I'm not a young man anymore. There isn't exactly a heavy workload at the moment, but there is a lot of responsibility. I don't want to discuss my salary, but I would just like to say that it isn't being paid, or rather it isn't being paid regularly. I think it is only fair I should have some guarantee of compensation when things start to look up."

Petrus suddenly threw back his head, so that the skin was stretched taut over the brittle bones of his face. For a brief moment, Larsen was convinced that the head was floating far out of the gloom of the office, somewhere in a realm of intolerable reason, an ancient, lost world. Petrus stuck his thumbs in his waistcoat pockets and thrust his face towards Larsen. A trace of his earlier disdain persisted: the touch of mocking pity a man feels who has resigned himself to the need for compromise.

"It's not my problem whether the wages in the yard are or are not paid. Señor Galvez is our administrator — see him about it."

"Galvez," Larsen repeated, with relief. He felt reprieved, felt the warm stirrings of convalescence flowing through him. "He's the one who gave them the certificate, the one who made the accusation."

"Quite right," Petrus agreed. "So much the worse for him. I should like to know what steps you took to replace him. I hope you don't imagine that a concern like the shipyard can function properly without expert, reliable managers. You did dismiss him, didn't you?"

How I'd love to throw my arms round him, risk my life for him, lend him ten times more money than he could possibly need, Larsen thought. He took off his coat, then replied: "Galvez, the administrator, brought charges then vanished. Or rather, he took good care to disappear beforehand. He sent me a letter of resignation three days ago. I understood at once that I should dismiss him. I looked all over Puerto Astillero for him, then I came down to Santa Maria. I was planning to dismiss him with this. But he hasn't shown up."

He slid the revolver on to the desktop, leaned back to admire it. "It's a Smith & Wesson," he said with an incongruous remnant of faded pride.

They both sat for a while in silence, staring at the perfect shape of the weapon, the faint lilac sheen given off by the barrel, the butt's rough black surface. They examined it, with no intention of touching it, exactly as though it were an animal whose existence they had heard of but never seen, an insect which had just landed on the desk, unaware that it was threatening and threatened, quite still, incomprehensible, perhaps trying to communicate by a quivering of its wings that was out of the range of human hearing.

"Put that away," Petrus ordered him, settling back in his chair. "It is not a method I am personally in favour of. It wouldn't do any good now. And how did you manage to bring a revolver into prison? Weren't you searched?"

"No. It didn't cross their minds or mine."

"That's incredible. So anyone could come in here and kill me. Even that man Galvez, who came I don't know how many times yesterday and the day before, asking to see me. I didn't want to see him, I've nothing to say to him. He's far more dead than if you had used that revolver on him."

"So he was here? Galvez? Are you sure? He can't be far away then. I have to find him. Not to put a bullet in him: that was just an impulse, the need to do something. But I'd like to spit in his face or take my time insulting him until I tire of it."

"I understand," Petrus lied in a firm voice. "Now put that revolver away and forget the whole thing. Find a capable and honest man for the administrator's job. You set his pay and conditions. Always bear in mind that, come what may, the shipyard must keep going."

"Agreed," Larsen replied, still staring at the revolver. Before he put it back in his coat he gently stroked the base of the butt with one finger.

(At first, with the first women and the first premonitions of importance and danger glimpsed in the pavilions of suburban meeting places, of improvised, ephemeral, social, recreational or sports clubs, it had been a snub-nosed .32, that he could carry in his waist pocket. That had been his adolescent love, polished, vaselined, inspected regularly at night. Next had come a Colt, bought for next-to-nothing from a conscript: weighty, enormous, indomitable. Useless as well, never brought out except at picnics, for target practice at a can or tree; standing there in shirt-sleeves, a cigarette dangling from his mouth, a glass of vermouth and rum in his left hand, waiting for the barbecue to be ready. Also on a few perfect days, with an endless blue sky, a tiny cart reduced to a seemingly motionless speck in the distance, the smell of smoke and chicken coops, a Slav settler. The age of maturity, when a man's a man. A pistol too big for his hand, forcing him to walk lopsided, its ever-present weight pressing against his ribs. Useful only to show and show off with as night fell and they grew weary of poker. He would get them to dismantle it and, blindfolded, choking on the cigarette some woman kept putting to his lips, he would re-assemble it, sightless, a ripple of friendly astonishment all round him, rejoicing at his fingers' loving, agile memory, bursting with pride as everyone applauded when he completed the trick by screwing the wooden panels with their rearing colt on to the sides of the revolver butt.)

"I agree with you completely," Larsen concurred, doing up his coat. "The shipyard must keep going at all costs. I won't hesitate to take all the steps necessary. We can sort out the wages later. But I must insist that it is extremely important for me to have some guarantee for the future."

Petrus raised his hands, then stroked his chin. He leaned forward, a discreet smile of triumph on his sallow face.

"I quite understand," he whispered. "You want to make sure your sacrifices are rewarded. I quite agree. As far as wages for now go, appoint an administrator and settle it with him. As for the future, what is it you require exactly?"

"Some sort of security, a contract, a document of some kind," Larsen gave a soft, tame, consoling laugh.

"That should present no problem," Petrus exclaimed excitedly. He unzipped his briefcase with a measured, practised gesture. "I think there should be no problem in our reaching an agreement." He took out some sheets of paper, reached for a pen in his waistcoat pocket. "What kind of document would you like? A five-year contract? Wait a second." He felt for his glasses in the inside pocket of his jacket, put them on and gave a slightly contemptuous, challenging smile. "It's up to you."

"All right," Larsen smiled back in a friendly way. "I want to take my time so I get it right. Let's see, yes — a contract, for five years, seems about right; I don't want to be tied forever. As for my salary . . . you must realise that the position of General Manager implies a certain lifestyle."

"Quite right. And I'd be the first to require it of you," Petrus' upturned face reflected an austere content. "What is your current salary? I must confess that more important matters have prevented me from scrutinising the shipyard's monthly payroll of late."

"Let's say it's . . . well, I earn four thousand at the moment. Let's call it six thousand from the day that things are back to normal."

"Six thousand?" Petrus paused, rubbing the tip of his pen across his lips. "Six thousand . . . I see no objection to that. But you'll have to earn it. Fine; I'll write you a provisional contract, establishing your position and the payments due to you for the next five years. We can draw up a proper contract later."

He bent over to write, tracing each letter carefully. An advertising loudspeaker van blared slogans in the silence, then droned into the distance. Larsen stood up and looked around. Planks of wood, tins, abandoned paintbrushes; the colour of the air charged with stillness, imminence; the old man sprawled over his desk. And beyond these visible signs, but pressing in on them, the silence of that old, almost unchanging part of the city. The huge horse, caught at the moment of lifting its hooves to break into a gallop, its waving tail, its colour that of autumnal grass. A damp, circular square with its confusion of tree branches; empty benches; puddles no one would watch drying out. An evening spreading up from the river, from the newly painted blocks of the commercial district.

"Read this," Petrus said.

Larsen picked up the piece of stiff cartridge paper and examined the flowery, even, perfect handwriting. "This document confirms my appointment of señor E. Larsen as General Manager of the shipyards belonging to Jeremias Petrus Ltd., of which I am chairman of the board of directors. This appointment will be for a period of five years, to be stipulated in a contract . . ."

Larsen folded the piece of card and put it in his pocket. Petrus stood up.

"Now everything is in order," Larsen said. "I never doubted you; but it's important to consider the legal side of things as well. You are a gentleman. I won't take up any more of your time; I think the sooner I'm back in Puerto Astillero the better. I may pay you another visit before I leave, to say goodbye."

"That won't be necessary," Petrus replied. "I want to take all the advantage I can of this period of rest. I still have a few details to work out."

"Fine." Larsen did not hold out his hand; nor did the old man. He turned at the door: Petrus seemed to have forgotten him already; he was seated again, spreading various documents out on the desk. "Excuse me," Larsen said, raising his voice. "I'm curious and flattered that you remember my name. My christian name, at least the initial."

Petrus looked up at him fleetingly, then spoke into his papers and briefcase.

"The inspector is a very decent man. He comes to visit me from time to time, we've even had lunch together. We've talked about a lot of things. He knew you were up in Puerto Astillero and that you had been to see me in the city. He showed me your file. You've hardly changed at all you know; a bit heavier perhaps, a bit older."

Larsen opened and shut the door without a word. At the end of the corridor he found the old man with the cardigan. He gave him a few pesos and followed him out to the armed policeman. From there, shivering with cold, he made his way slowly and silently along the tiles until he emerged into the street.

He crossed the freezing circle of the Plaza del Fundador and walked towards the city centre down a street with leprous walls, nearly all of them covered with the dried spindrift of creepers; a street of walled gardens and large old houses; of shadows and absences. *Perhaps I've never been in this part of the city before, perhaps everything would have been different, perhaps I've always longed to live in a house like this.* He walked along erect, his heels clicking, seeking out the quieter spots to make his footsteps resound, determined not to let himself be defeated, yet unsure of what there was left for him to defend.

Why not? Everything might have been different if, five years ago, I had been the sort of man who walked through the old quarters of Santa

Maria late in the afternoon. Simply for the pleasure of strolling along these lonely streets and welcoming night as it descended from the heights of the new square, in no hurry to get anywhere, with no concern for work or misfortune, thinking, idly at first and then in a friendly way, of the lives of the dead who once inhabited these houses with their marble steps and wrought-iron gates. It's possible. Anyway, now more than ever I must do something, anything.

In the middle of the new square, while he was hesitating over the choice of where to eat and sleep, he realised he must above all guard himself against the temptation of not returning to Puerto Astillero. "I can't see myself in any other place on earth. I can't do anything else, be concerned about the outcome."

He walked down towards the port. He ate without noticing what he was eating, agreed a price for a room for the night. He was stirring his coffee, thinking about a waiting-room for death, a blessed period of adjustment, when the idea came to him.

At first he was astonished he hadn't thought of it before, at the very moment when Petrus said: "That Galvez man, who came I don't know how many times yesterday and the day before to see me." Now Larsen felt an overriding need to be with Galvez, to look on the friendly face of someone connected with the logical world in which Larsen could no longer breathe. Like him, Galvez must be wandering around Santa Maria, a stranger, an outsider, perplexed by the language and customs, his troubles magnified by exile. He imagined their meeting, their talk, all the references they could make to their own land, the superfluous but consoling exchange of memories, their spontaneous contempt for the barbarians.

Soon he was thinking of the Santa Maria of five years before, of all the time he had had to wait, the months of his triumph, then the catastrophe that was as predictable as it was unjust. Out of the whirl of people, nights and events, he hit on his only chance of reaching Galvez: the tall, bulky, gruff, almost-human figure of officer Medina. Perhaps he was still in the city. Larsen went over to the telephone and half-heartedly dialled the number.

"Police Headquarters," said a sleepy voice.

"To speak with Medina." Larsen could hear the hesitation and then silence, different, definite. He smiled in encouragement as he tried to rescue Medina from his memory, to imagine him scornful and suspicious, to will him into being alive and still part of the police force.

"Police Headquarters," a second, more alert voice said.

"This is a friend of Medina's. I've just arrived in the city."

"Who's speaking?"

"Larsen, that's what he knows me as. A friend from years back. Could you tell him, please?"

He could hear a distant, night-time creaking, then a shallow kind of silence, empty as a wall, followed by a different silence, this time taut and filled with the hum of a large, busy room.

"Medina," growled a bored voice.

"Larsen here, I don't know if you remember me." He immediately regretted his enthusiasm, his nervous self-satisfaction. He gave a cringing smile to disarm the other's caution.

"Larsen," the voice eventually said, as if with a sigh. "Larsen," it said again, surprised and happy.

"Inspector?"

"Deputy. About to retire. Where are you speaking from?"

"A fish restaurant down by the river. Between the harbour and the factory."

"Wait a minute." (*I'm not trying to escape; unfortunately, I've nothing to lose, nothing can happen to me now*). "The problem is Larsen that I can't leave here until morning. I'm glad you called; why don't you come and see me, for old times' sake? If you walk up to the promenade you're bound to find a taxi. If not, take the B bus, that will drop you in the square opposite Police Headquarters. Will you come?"

Larsen agreed and hung up. *What can they do to me? I haven't even got any enemies left. Nobody is going to set a trap or lay hands on me. I've nothing to fear, I can chat and amuse them.*

Medina was sitting under the glare of neon lighting in an empty office. The air in the room was hazy from tobacco smoke; dirty coffee cups were strewn over the tables and bookshelves. Medina sat back with his gangling legs up on the desk, smiling as he twiddled his thumbs above his stomach. His face was just as Larsen remembered it; the pockmarks prevented any wrinkles showing; his hair was flecked with a narrow band of grey from his temples to the nape of the neck. *This place was full of men and he got rid of them. 'I want to be alone in here.' What use can I be to him?*

They talked of the old days, though neither of them mentioned the whorehouse. Medina smiled indulgently, as if recalling hard times full of hope. Then he yawned and slowly pulled himself upright. He stood up, stretching his huge body in the brown uniform, heavier now, but still young.

"Larsen," he repeated. He looked thoughtfully down at the man hunched in the leather armchair who had put on a silly, defensive grin, and from time to time scratched at a grey lock of hair dangling down his forehead. "It's true, I've been wanting to talk to you. We know that you've been in Puerto Astillero for the past few months, working there."

What game have you invented to astonish me, to make sure I can't forget the distance between us?

"That's right," he replied unhurriedly, with a hint of disdain, a show of vanity. "You've been well informed. I live there, in the Belgrano Hotel. I work in Petrus' shipyard. I'm the manager. We're trying our best to reorganise the yard. That's all my cards on the table. Anyway, you know I never tried to hide anything."

Medina's teeth glinted. He shook his head, then the words came tumbling out in his gruff voice: "And you know I never had anything against you personally. When the governor said 'Enough!'

we had to obey orders. That seems like a hundred years ago. I'm pleased you thought of calling me. And if there's anything I can do for you . . ." He walked back to the desk and perched on the edge. "Would you like some coffee? That's all I can offer you here. I've already had more than my share. Like I told you, I reached the rank of deputy inspector, and that's it. I'm retiring within the year." His face came alive when he smiled, his body athletic, reconciled to his fate. "Ask whatever you like. I'm sure you didn't call just for the pleasure of seeing me again."

"That's true," Larsen admitted. He crossed his legs, balanced his hat on his knee. "You must have known that as soon as I rang, as soon as you recognised my voice. I only need a small favour. It concerns an employee at the shipyard. Galvez, one of the managers. He disappeared a few days ago. He sent me a letter of resignation posted in Santa Maria. Naturally enough, his wife is very worried. I offered to come and look for him, but I can't find a trace of him in the whole city. I thought of coming to see if you knew anything before I went back. Imagine having to go back to his wife with no news at all."

Medina paused for a moment, flicked his wrist to look at his watch, then pushed himself upright from the desk. His rubber-soled shoes squeaked on the linoleum floor as he came over to Larsen. He stood over him, almost brushing against his knees. He thrust his mottled face, with its old weary expression of cruelty and boredom, down at Larsen.

"What else, Larsen?" An impatient edge had crept into his voice. "What else? I've got other things to see to before I leave, and I'm tired. What else do you know about this man Galvez?"

"What else?" Larsen mused. "I've got nothing to hide." He lifted his hands and stared at the palms with a smile. He wasn't frightened; the question brought memories of all the other men who had leaned over him asking that: "What else? You could say they're trade secrets. But I'm sure I'm right to trust you. Galvez came to Santa Maria to bring charges against señor Petrus. Petrus was arrested, and as you know he's now here in this building. I spoke to him this afternoon, and he told me Galvez had tried to see him several times. That's all. I thought, reasonably enough, that if Galvez had been here you would know where he could be found. What else? Nothing. There's nothing else you can get from me, because that's all I have."

Up above him, Medina nodded, and smiled once more. Then he let his breath out slowly, and began to button up his jacket. He yawned sleepily, looked at his watch again.

"Come on Larsen, let's go. I believe what you're saying, I'm sure you know nothing else. Come with me, and I'll tell you the rest."

They left the office and walked along the tiled corridors.

Beneath a dim light, a policemen saluted and clicked his heels. Medina flung open a door.

"Go in," he said, in an annoyed, taunting tone. "I'm afraid I can't ask you to choose, beggars can't be choosers."

They walked a few steps through the dimly lit chill with its smell of disinfectant, then stopped by a dentist's chair with behind it two glass cases full of rows of gleaming metal, one on either side of a broken radiator. They skirted a small roll-top desk, then just by the back wall of the ever colder room, up against the steel filing cabinets, surrounded with water trickling through gutters in the floor, they came to a table covered in a stiff white cloth. Medina lifted it, then had to fumble for his handkerchief to stifle a sneeze.

"This is the rest of the story," he said. "It's Galvez, isn't it? Have a look and tell me quickly, before you catch cold. Is it him? I'm not trying to rush you."

Larsen felt no hatred or pity for the white face on the slab, hard, impenetrable, relieved of all its additions, the slightly obscene shiny moistness of its rolled-up eyes. *It's as I always said: now he has lost that smile of his, he always had this face underneath the other one, all the time he was trying to convince us he was alive, all the time he was dying of boredom with an already lost, pregnant woman, two sharp-nosed dogs, Kunz and myself, the infinite mud, the shadow of the shipyard, the vulgarity of hope. Now at last he is showing the serious face of a real man, a harshness, a glow he would never have dared cast on life. All that's left of his shortsighted gaze are those puffy eyelids, the halfmoons of his shallow gaze. But he's not to blame for that.*

"Yes, it's him. What happened?"

"Nothing to it. He got on the ferry; as it was going past Latorre island he threw himself in. It took half an hour, but by sunset his body was washed up by the jetty. I knew it was Galvez, but I wanted to show him to you."

He sneezed again. He put a hand on Larsen's shoulder, with the other quickly pulled the cloth back up over the dead man's face.

"That's all," Medina said. "Just sign a statement for me, and you can go."

He led him down the gloomy corridors, showed him into a room where two men were playing chess. All of a sudden he lost all semblance of the cordiality he had shown up to now.

"Tosar," he said. "This person has just identified the drowned man. Add whatever he has to say to the file, and then let him go."

One of the men pulled a typewriter across the desk in front of him. The other looked dully in Larsen's direction, then went back to studying the chess-board. Medina crossed the room and went out by the far door without looking round or saying goodbye.

Smiling, well pleased that he had been so clever, Larsen sat down without waiting to see if they offered him a chair. He had just decided that Galvez had not died, that he was not going to fall into such a childish trap, that at dawn he would return to the unchanging world of Puerto Astillero, the bearer of no news.

The Shipyard vii

The Summerhouse v

The House i

The Cabin vii

Then came Larsen's last journey up-river to the shipyard. By then he was not simply alone but terror-struck, caught in the first uncertain glimmer of lucidity of those who, against their will but without any vanity or calculation, come to suspect their own need to believe. He knew little; he sneered at everything else around him that wanted to be known.

He was irredeemably, unspectacularly alone. He took slow, reluctant, unhurried steps across a territory whose map shrank by the hour, all possibility or desire for choice long since gone. He had the problem — he, his bones, his bulk, his shadow's problem — to arrive on time at the unknown, forever fixed place and moment. He was promised (by no one) that the appointment would be kept.

Nothing more then than a man, this one, Larsen, heading up-river in some boat or other, at the sudden fall of a winter's night, staring absent-mindedly or to distract himself at what little could still be seen of the riverbank undergrowth, his right ear taking in the calls of birds with unknown names.

So without knowing more than he could bear to, but at least having discovered at some point in his voyage what he had been searching for from the window of Petrus' jail facing the Plaza del Fundador, he arrived at Puerto Astillero just as a green ray sank below the horizon. He went into Belgrano's to comfort himself with the sense of order brought by taking things in stages, to have a wash and a drink, to persuade the owner he was no ghost.

He went up to his room; then shivering, intimidated by the cold, groped along the dark corridor to wash at the handbasin. He stood there in shirt-sleeves, the only sound the cheerful gurgle of the water. As he raised his face to dry it, he felt the thin, biting air on his cheeks. He looked for the moon but could see nothing more than its wan silvery glow. It was then he truly accepted he was dead. Pressed against the basin, he finished drying his fingers and the back of his neck, curious but at peace, with no concern for dates, guessing at what he might do to fill in the time until the end, until the distant day when his death would no longer be a merely private event.

He finished dressing. He was bored with examining the revolver, snapping it open, peering into the empty drum as he spun it round, counting the bullets lined up on the table like toy soldiers. He was dressed and combed, freshly washed in the parts not concealed by his clothes. He sat there, shaved and perfumed, one elbow on the table as he lifted a cigarette to his mouth without drawing in any smoke. Chilled to the bone, he sat alone in the centre of this tiny room which the lack of furniture made seem almost normal size. His past was gone, and he knew that he or anybody else could equally well perform the actions of the inevitable future. He was happy, though it was a useless happiness. The boy asked if he could come in.

Larsen did not turn to look at him: he remembered well enough his narrow forehead, wiry black hair, the tranquil but alert expression on the boy's face.

"I thought I heard you call. How have you been all this time? They said you'd never come back. I came to ask if you're eating here. The ferry brought fresh meat."

As he spoke, he flicked his duster at the bedside table and the shelf with its alarm clock; then he came over to dust the corners of the table.

"Look," Larsen said, "there's no way I'm going to eat the garbage they cook here."

"Fine," the boy agreed enthusiastically. "But there is fresh meat. I couldn't give a damn whether you eat here or not." He bent and wiped one of the table legs, then straightened, smiling, but still without looking at Larsen.

"Look," Larsen began again. He dropped the cigarette on the floor and cocked his head at the boy in astonishment. "What are you doing here anyway? I mean what are you after, staying on here in Puerto Astillero, this stinking place?"

The boy paid him no heed. He didn't seem to credit that the words were addressed to him. He leaned against the table and slowly lifted the filthy rag he used as a duster, handkerchief and towel. He took it by the corners between thumb and first finger and flourished it in front of a broad grin which revealed gleaming white teeth.

"I could ask you the same. With more reason. What are you hoping for from here? It's been a long time, and nothing you wanted has happened. Or so it seems to me."

"Ah!" Larsen said, rubbing his hands together.

The boy backed away from the table, and twirled two dance steps, wrapping the duster round his head.

"That stupid old woman will be shouting for me, you'll see."

"Ah!" Larsen repeated. Looking up, his face was skewed in a mixture of thought and admiration. He felt the need for a tiny act of treachery, as one might need a tonic or a shot of liquor. "So you don't want to understand. Fetch the talc and shine my shoes."

Still dancing, the boy went to the wardrobe and brought over an oval-shaped tin with a pattern of blue flowers on a bright yellow background. He knelt to sprinkle the shoes that Larsen casually pushed out towards him, then polished them with the cloth. All that could be seen of him was his shiny hair, his worn white jacket with holes showing a woollen vest beneath.

"So you don't want to understand, my boy." Larsen rolled the words out slowly and sonorously to make them last.

He waited for him to put the talc away and lock the wardrobe door. Then he walked slowly over, sure the boy would not move. He cupped his face in his hand, shook him, then let him go. The boy did not budge, but looked down and away, folding and unfolding the cloth at shoulder height.

"That's by way of explanation, so you can't help but understand." Larsen's words were a slow, weary drawl. "An honest man touched your face. Remember that. I knew a kid like you once, he even looked like you, who sold flowers early mornings on Corrientes, in a world you know nothing of. Flowers for performers, whores, kept women. Violets were his speciality, as I recall. One night years later when I was back in circulation I was sitting at a table in a café with someone and the kid came over to our table with his basket of violets. Two cops who got served drinks at the back pawed him laughing as they went past, one on the way in, the other on his way out. I don't know if you get my drift. I'm talking to you like a father. I reckon what I just told you is the worst that could happen to anyone."

Larsen picked up his hat from the table and put it on in front of the mirror, trying to whistle an old tango whose title and words he had forgotten. The boy had flitted over to the bed and was busy wiping the window-frame with his crumpled duster.

"That's how things are," Larsen said dolefully. He unbuttoned his coat, took out his wallet and counted out five ten peso notes. He tossed them on the table: "Take this. Fifty pesos as a gift. What I owe you is besides that. But don't tell the boss I give money away."

"Thanks a lot," the boy said, drifting over. "So you won't be eating with us. I have to tell them." His voice had a harder edge to it, more insolent, breathless.

"A few years back instead of giving you advice I'd have smashed your face in. Remember what I told you? He came over with his sprays of violets; it was winter then too. When the cops touched him, he couldn't hide it, everyone had seen. He couldn't get mad because they were the law. So he did the saddest thing in the world: he smiled at us with a smile I hope to God you'll never have on your face."

"Right," the boy replied, blinking, looking almost happy. He had spread the cloth over the table, and was pressing on it with both hands. His dark features had taken on a childish expression, and his slanting eyes, his half open mouth a mixture of dreaminess and vague mistrust, a suppressed desire to ask questions.

"Will you be back very late? I'll have some food kept for you if you want. Hey, I forgot. This came for you. Yesterday I think."

He looked down and rummaged in his filthy trouser pocket, pulled out a folded, opened envelope.

Larsen read the lilac sheet of paper: "Expecting you for dinner up in the house with Josefina at 8.30 p.m. But come earlier. Your A.I."

"Good news?" the boy asked.

Larsen left without replying or turning to look at him. In the bar downstairs he refused a drink with the owner; instead he rushed out into the cold of the street. He turned right and set off down the wide road lined with bare trees, the still invisible moon making a pretence of guiding him with its faint white glow. He walked block after block without thinking. (It was not a thought, this image of himself scurrying along not merely to the gate, to the dark, frozen hump of the summerhouse, to the garden with the chalky blur of its statues, the footpaths overgrown with weeds, the stakes and withered stems of the flower beds. No, this time he was heading through the cold to the the very heart of the house as well, raised high above any possible flood. To the warmth and heady crackle of flames in the chimney of the huge living-room; to the the oldest, most venerable of the armchairs, the one reserved for the weight of Petrus, or the deceased mother, or the aunt with an unpronouncable name who was also dead.)

Scurrying along, seeing himself hasten along towards the centre of a warm, clean and tidy room, towards a scene over which he would preside proudly and naturally, he acknowledged, especially to begin with, all his misconceptions about it, as he planned the changes he would bring in to satisfy the historic need to define the start of a new era, one of his own making.

He rang the bell and waited, watching as the tip of the moon climbed out of the shadow of the trees, emerging above a haystack, or some decaying villa down by the homesteads he had never visited. Then, as in fairy stories of which he remembered only the magical sensation of a whole series of obstacles being overcome, Larsen slipped through the gate, past the silent Josefina who did not return his greeting, past the bounding dog, and tried to walk loud and firmly down the twisting gravel path, dodging the branches grabbing at his face, trying desperately to construe a welcome from the white shapes reflecting the moon and the pond's elegiac smell.

He stopped at the entrance to the summerhouse, the woman's footsteps and the panting dog at his back.

"We weren't expecting you," Josefina said, with an impatient cackle that was distant allusion to a laugh. "His lordship vanishes without a word, then turns up completely unannounced."

Larsen stood at the arched doorway to the summerhouse, staring at the cement table and the chairs inside. Hands in his pockets, his body twisted to one side, he waited for the moon to climb a little higher over his right shoulder.

"It's late," the woman said. "I don't know why I came down to open up."

Larsen felt Angelica Ines' message in his pocket, but left it where it was. Up in the house, two windows shone with a golden light.

"Come back tomorrow if you like. It's very late." He recognised the mocking challenge in her voice.

"Tell her I'm here. She sent me a note inviting me to dinner at the house."

"I know. That was three days ago. I took the message to Belgrano's. But now she's in bed, she's ill."

"That doesn't matter. I had to go to Santa Maria. Señor Petrus sent for me. Tell her I've brought news from her father. I have to talk to her, even if only for a few minutes."

The woman repeated the sound which vaguely recalled a laugh. Head thrown back, Larsen was staring up at the lights of the house, anxious only to obliterate the time keeping him from the moment he set foot on what was his by right, when he could settle in a high-backed wooden armchair by the hearth, home at last.

"She's ill, I tell you. She can't come down, and you can't go up there. You'd better leave, I have to lock up."

Hesitant, Larsen turned slowly round, kindling his hatred. He saw the tiny woman, her face drenched in moonlight, smiling at him through taut lips.

"I was thinking you'd never come back," she murmured.

"I've brought a message from her father. A really important one. Are we going up?"

The woman took a step forward. She waited for his words and a second later their meaning to coalesce then fade away, like shadows in the white night air. Then she gave a real, stifled, challenging laugh. Larsen understood, or perhaps not himself exactly, more like his memory, something that had remained curled up alive inside him. He stretched out a hand. It brushed the woman's throat and came to rest on her shoulder. He could hear the dog growl and stir.

"She's ill; she must be asleep already," Josefina said. She scarcely moved, careful not to frighten his hand away, forcing him instead to increase its pressure. "So you don't want to leave? Aren't you cold out here?"

"It is cold," Larsen agreed.

Still smiling, her tiny, gleaming eyes turned up to him, the woman stroked the dog to reassure it. She moved closer to Larsen, keeping his hand on her shoulder as tightly as if she were holding it there. And then he leaned down to kiss her, another vague memory, his lips acknowledging desire and peace.

"Idiot." She said. "What took you so long? Idiot."

Larsen nodded slowly. He stared at her as if he had always known her mocking, glittering eyes, her large, nondescript mouth which now revealed her teeth in the moonlight. Tossing her head from side to side, the woman calculated in astonished delight how stupid men can be, how absurd life is. She kissed him again.

Guided by his hand, Larsen rounded the boundary of the summerhouse in the centre of the garden, brushed past the naked statues, discovered new smells of plants, dampness, the bread oven, the huge whispering bird-cage. At last he reached the tiled house floor, enclosed in the concrete foundation separating the rooms from the earth and the water. The woman Josefina's bedroom was level with the garden.

Larsen smiled in the shadows. *That's us, the poor*, he thought resignedly. Josefina switched on the light, showed him in, took his hat. Larsen could not bring himself to look round the room as she bustled about in front of him, tidying things or hiding them. He stood there, the old, forgotten spark of youth suffusing his face along with an equally old, awkward and lascivious smile, as he smoothed the lock of sparse grey hair down over his forehead.

"Make yourself at home," she said calmly, without looking at him. "I'll just see if she needs anything and be back. Our crazy one."

She left quickly, closing the door without a sound. At that moment, Larsen felt that all the cold which had seeped into his body that day and for the whole of the draining, final winter in the shipyard had finally lodged in his bones and from now on would forever give off its icy chill, wherever he might be. This only increased his smile and his wish to forget. He began to examine the maid's room with avid enthusiasm. He moved rapidly round it, touching some of the objects, picking others up to look at them more closely, with a sense of consolation that made up for his sadness, like someone sniffing the air of his home land before he dies. There, once more, were the metal bed with its loose metal frame that would clank beneath the thrusting bodies; the green china washing bowl and jug with their embossed pattern of broad aquatic leaves; the mirror bordered with stiff, yellowing tulle; the cheap prints of virgins and saints; photos of comedians and singers; a pencil drawing of a dead old woman in a thick oval frame. The smell too, the indelible mixture of an unaired room, woman, fried food, powders and perfumes, the cheap length of cloth rolled in the wardrobe.

It was when she returned, carrying two bottles of light-coloured wine and a glass, sighing as she pushed the door shut with her leg to shield him from the biting cold, the dog's claws and whines, the many wasted years, that Larsen knew that this was when he should really be afraid. It seemed to him he had been forced to become himself again, to return to the abrupt truth he had been in adolescence. He was young again, in a room which might have been his or his mother's, with a woman who was his equal. He could marry her, hit her, walk out; whatever he did would not alter the sense of fellow-feeling, the deep and solid bond between them.

"That was a good idea; pour me a drink," he said, at last willing to sit on the edge of the bed.

He drank with her from the only glass, trying to get her drunk while he responded to the torrent of lies, questions and reproaches so often heard with the absent, lofty smile he had been given to use for a few hours. Later he said: "Keep quiet," removed the jug with its leaves and flowers from the bowl, and burnt the passport to happiness that old man Petrus had signed for him.

He did not want to think about the woman sleeping upstairs, in the land he had promised himself. He allowed Josefina to undress him, but continued to demand silence the whole night long even while he acknowledged the community of flesh, the woman's candid desire.

He left in the early hours, whispering all the required promises. He took her arm and, flanked by her and the dog, crossed the tremendous moonless silence of the garden. Neither before nor after their last kiss would he turn to look at the outline of the house beyond his reach. When he got to the end of the avenue, he turned right and began to walk back towards the yard. By now, in those circumstances, he was no longer Larsen or anyone else. The night with the woman had been a trip to the past, someone called up in a spiritualist session, a smile, a scrap of comfort, a mist that anyone else could just as well have met.

He felt the need to walk to the shipyard to have a last look at the huge dark cube. Then he made a silent detour to snoop around the cabin where Galvez had lived with his wife. He could smell embers from the eucalyptus fire, trod on the previous night's remains. He crouched down and sat on a box, then lit a cigarette. He sat hunched, immobile at this highest point in the world, and was aware of being at the centre of a perfect solitude he had so often imagined, and almost desired, in far-off years.

First he heard a noise, followed at once by a violent yellow light through the geometric slits in the planks of the cabin walls. At first the sound was a confused angry yowling of puppies, then, as he made the mistake of listening more closely, it became human, almost comprehensible, a string of curses. The strange light told him more than the stifled, continuous howl; he shut his eyes so as not to see it, and went on smoking until he burnt his fingers. Him, someone, an anonymous bundle in this summit of a frozen night, trying not to be, trying to convert his solitude into absence.

He stood up stiffly, and went across to the cabin, dragging his feet. He raised himself up until he reached the neatly sawn hole in the wall that served as a window, covered by bits of glass, pieces of cardboard, rags.

He could see the woman half-naked on the bed, bleeding, pushing with all her might, fingers clawing at her furiously, rhythmically shaking head. He saw the amazing round belly, caught the sudden glint of her glazed eyes and clenched teeth. It took him some time to understand and then he recognised the trap. Trembling with fear and disgust he moved away from the window and started to walk towards the river. Muddy, half-running, he went past the still sleeping Belgrano's, and a few minutes later came to the planks of the jetty. Through his tears he could smell the invisible vegetation, timber, stagnant puddles.

The boatmen woke him before dawn under the sign PUERTO ASTILLERO. He discovered they were heading north; they were happy to take his watch as payment for his passage. Huddled in the stern, he waited for them to finish loading. It was daylight by the time they started the engine and shouted their farewells. Sunk in his overcoat, anxious, chilled to the bone, Larsen was dreaming of a sunny scene in which Josefina was playing with the dog, while Petrus' daughter waved a hand languidly in the background. As the light brightened, he looked down at his hands: he studied the shape of their wrinkles, saw how readily the veins stood out. He struggled to turn his head and as the boat veered and slid out into midstream, he contemplated the swift ruin of the shipyard, its walls' silent collapse. Deaf to the launch's throbbing engine, his keen ear could make out the faint sound of moss climbing over the piles of bricks, of rust eating at the iron.

(Or better: the boatmen found him. They almost stepped on his black, hunched body, his head on his knees protected by the greasy prestige of his hat, soaked in dew, delirious. He shouted that he had to escape, brandishing his revolver despairingly. They punched him in the mouth. Then one of them felt sorry for him; they picked him out of the mud, gave him a swig of liquor, laughing, slapping his back. They made as though to clean off his clothes, his dark uniform, frayed by adversity, stretched by his bulk. There were three of them; their names are recorded. In the chill of early morning they went certain and unhurriedly to and fro between the boat and the small warehouse, loading goods, swearing at each other good-naturedly. Larsen offered them his watch; they admired it but refused to take it. Careful not to humiliate him, they helped him climb on board and settle on the bench in the stern. As the engine set the boat quivering Larsen, wrapped in the dry sacks they had thrown him, could picture in detail the destruction of the yard's buildings, could hear the hiss of corrosion and collapse. But the hardest thing for him to bear must have been the unmistakable, frolicsome air of September, the first faint smell of a southern spring seeping irresistibly in through the crevices of an exhausted winter. He sniffed at the air, licking his split lip as the speeding boat made its way up-river. He died of pneumonia in Rosario before the week was out. His real name appears in full on the hospital register.)